MW01178856

Praise for The Fountain
Book 1 in The Fountain Series

"The Fountain is not your ordinary YA boarding school novel. With magic, mystery and romance woven together in just the right measure, it is sure to be a 'must read' with teens everywhere."
 - Jacqueline Guest, author of Ghost Messages
   and The Comic Book War

"Suzy Vadori does wonders with taking a simple theme - making a wish - and turning it into a wonderful novel of rich dialogue, memorable characters, and a few twists and turns, that will have the reader immersed in this mystery-laced read, bringing together both past and present, right and wrong, and of course, how one wish creates a ripple effect that may never be undone."
 - Avery Olive, author of A Stiff Kiss
   and Won't Let Go

"The Fountain is a very enjoyable book that can be read by readers from 10 to 100!"
 - Kristina Anderson, The Avid Reader

Wall of Wishes

Suzy Vadori

Old Vines Press

Old Vines Press

Published by Old Vines Press, 24 Wentworth Manor SW, Calgary, AB T3H 5K5, Canada

Wall of Wishes, Copyright © 2020 by Suzy Vadori.

Edited by Simon Rose.

Cover by Jeff Minkevics, copyright © 2020 by Jeff Minkevics.

Interior design and layout by Michell Plested.

Print version set in Cambria; titles in Cambria, byline in Cambria.

Published in Canada

Printed in Canada

Library and Archives Canada Cataloguing in Publication

Vadori, Suzy, 1975-, author

Wall of Wishes / Suzy Vadori.

Electronic monograph issued in EPUB, MOBI, PDF and print format.

ISBN (pbk.) 978-1-7772009-0-9.

ISBN (Mobi) 978-1-7772009-3-0.

ISBN (ePub) 978-1-7772009-2-3.

ISBN (pdf) 978-1-7772009-1-6.

CHAPTER ONE

Ava

I dragged my hand along the cold stone of the St. Augustus hallway. The walls held secrets. Secrets I'd unleashed with my own selfishness. I'd made a careless wish that I'd carry with me forever. My hand shook as it trailed behind me.

I wish that St. Augustus had never heard of Courtney or her family.

The wish I'd made in the fall was never far from my thoughts. It colored every day I was here and I wanted to be free of it. My stomach churned. The feeling had followed me home at Christmas break. Or, at least to the home in my new reality.

The main building's hallways creeped in circles. I'd taken the long way to meet up with Ethan, who'd told me all about his great New Year's ski trip over text. I sighed. One day soon my guilt would stop gnawing at me from the inside out. Wouldn't it?

Who would I be if I'd never found the fountain? The question haunted me.

I wouldn't be the captain of the swim team. I might not even be dating Ethan and that I really couldn't imagine. He'd been my rock through all of this. It had been four months since my wish and although every day I wondered what alternate reality might have played out, I'd stopped hoping I could undo it. It had been too long. I was stuck.

The din of the foyer buzzed in my ears. Kids were laughing

and hugging their New Year's greetings in slow motion around me. Dull winter light spilled in through the tall lead-lined windows, casting shadows on the ornate ceiling frescos. I'd rehearsed this moment on the plane ride, although I couldn't keep the inevitable from happening. I closed my eyes.

As much as I wanted to see Ethan, Courtney might be here, in the foyer. I knew she'd been accepted to St. Augustus this semester. She was coming back. An agreeable Courtney. One whose dad hadn't come here for school and hadn't helped my dad graduate. A Courtney I couldn't quite wrap my head around. One I might be friends with, if circumstances were different.

Despite the fountain's power, I hadn't kept Courtney away forever. She'd come anyway, a year and a half later than she should have, yet she'd come.

I shuddered to think what this place might do to her. What it had done to her before. Would she become the Courtney I'd once known, in another life, whose green eyes were flecked with ice? My gut writhed as I searched for Ethan's dark shock of hair in the foyer. He'd said I'd erased history, which he didn't think was a big deal. But it was. My fists clenched at my sides. I was trapped in a loop I couldn't break out of.

"Ava!"

And then Courtney was there, weaving her way through the crowd of students. The sight of her red waves of hair pushed the breath from my lungs. I wasn't ready. I might never be ready. Every nightmare I'd had over the break bundled themselves into a smiling, unassuming Courtney. I stifled the urge to turn and run. It wouldn't help anyway. Besides, this Courtney didn't deserve that. Her curls bounced on her shoulders as she closed the distance between us. My lungs were on fire. I might never take another normal breath again.

"We can get out of here, if you want?" Ethan's voice was at my shoulder. His hand on the small of my back was a lifeline. I wanted to take it.

Alarms went off in my head, clanging their imaginary bells against my eardrums. My feet stayed rooted to the slate floor. I couldn't speak. Ethan slipped his arm around my waist, giving me strength. Courtney smiled so wide her back teeth were visible, like a wolf in sheep's clothing.

A montage of time-travel movies flashed through my mind, almost overwhelming my neural networks. My path was about to collide with Courtney's. There might be fireworks. Explosions. That was the first rule of mixing alternate timelines, wasn't it? It was all wrong and she had no idea. Telling her was out of the question. She'd never understand. My knees wobbled. Ethan's grip around my waist tightened.

"You met her before, at the swim meet, remember?" Ethan reminded me, in a low voice, as he spun me toward him. "The fountain's granted dozens of wishes going back almost a hundred years and the world hasn't imploded yet. Nothing bad is going to happen."

I studied his gleaming white running shoes. I didn't need to look at his face to know his mouth turned up in a half-laugh. He found the humor in every situation. I loved that about him.

"I'm Courtney. We met at the swim meet last fall."

I turned to face a bright-faced Courtney, who had her hand out to shake mine. She was introducing herself. I wanted to scream. When I didn't move to take her hand, she dropped hers. Her smile fell with it.

"Say something," Ethan whispered in my ear. He gave me a gentle nudge in the back, prodding me forward.

Gooseflesh crawled up my spine. Etiquette dictated that I should shake her hand, but my arms were pinned to my sides.

Courtney's forehead creased in a frown. I shrugged away from Ethan's protective shadow, steeling my legs. What was the worst that could happen if I ran out of here right now, effectively ending our interaction?

"Have I interrupted something?" asked Courtney, looking between Ethan and me.

"Not at all," Ethan said.

He took Courtney's hand and shook it, using an exaggerated pumping motion.

"You look very *familiar*," he said in an affected accent, featuring some sort of southern twang.

I nudged him in the ribs. What was he doing? He'd met her in her own yard. He'd gone looking for her in Boston after I'd wished her away. Was he going to pretend that was a coincidence? An accent was a thinner disguise than Superman's Clark Kent glasses.

"Oh?" Courtney blinked at him without recognition.

I narrowed my eyes. Ethan was a tough guy to forget, but maybe my lens was colored.

"Coach Laurel told me to find Ava. That's you, right?" Courtney smiled at me less brightly than she had before. "I just transferred from Boston. I swim. I mean, I swam there and I'd like to swim here."

I was frozen to the spot, watching her sputter.

"I get that the team was chosen in the fall, so I'd be happy as an alternate for the rest of the season. Coach said it would be up to the captain if I got to swim in meets. You're the captain, right?" Her upper lip twitched as she spoke.

Everything about this interaction was weird. A shiver ran through me. This was a chance to start again, with the slate wiped clean. I should jump at the chance.

I stared at her face, her skin pale and flawless, with an orderly splash of ginger freckles dotting her nose. Even her strawberry colored eyelashes were unassuming. She waited for my answer, her nose crinkled. She was going to think there was something wrong with me if I kept staring at her. Maybe there was something wrong with me. I reached for the heat of Ethan's hand, steadying myself. What was I supposed to say? Of course, you can have your spot back, Courtney. It's actually rightfully yours. You were supposed to be team captain too, before I wished you away. So, you can have that back too. No harm done. Can you ever forgive me?

Instead of saying any of those things, I let out an odd squeaking grunt, which sent Courtney's eyebrows up into her hairline.

"If you let me swim, I'll earn it, I promise. I don't expect special treatment." Her green eyes shifted from me to Ethan, then back again. I opened my mouth, but no words came out. How was

I going to see her every day? Shame roiled in my stomach. Shame for what I'd done. She could never find out.

"I hear your dad's a state senator," Ethan piped up.

My eyes widened at his left field comment. Was he as thrown as I was, for once? Courtney said she didn't want special treatment. Did she think I cared about who her dad was? What I had on my mind was much bigger than that. Ethan's flippant tone did nothing to calm the storm that swirled inside me, threatening to blow. Was he buying me time? I dropped his hand.

"He is. I'm sorry, have we met?" Courtney folded her arms.

"I think you and I spoke once, when I was visiting Boston," Ethan said, grinning like he'd just delivered the punchline to a joke. I swatted him in the leg. I wanted to get out of the foyer, but if I left who knew what he would say, how much he'd give away.

"Did we meet on the street, in front of my house?" Her face brightened. "You didn't say you went to St. Augustus. I would remember that."

"Yes, well - you never asked."

Ethan's smile washed over me without easing me the way it usually did.

"And you never called me," she chided.

Bile spiraled up the back of my throat. I imagined puking all over her crisp St. Augustus hoodie. She'd probably bought it at the school store that day. I hadn't asked what Ethan and Courtney had talked about when he'd met her in Boston. But she'd given Ethan her number and had waited for him to call. She flashed a warm smile his way. A hot flush flared into my cheeks. My hand shot out to take his, more firmly this time.

"I'll talk to Coach Laurel," I said, my voice tight. "We have to go."

"Bye!" Ethan waved to her as I tugged him away. I didn't wait to see Courtney's face.

"What was that about?" Ethan asked once we were safely out of the foyer.

I continued to pull at his hand, leading him to the breakfast bar in the cafeteria. Temper ran through my blood. Food might help me think. I let go of him to slice a multi-grain bagel, running a jagged knife back and forth as the bread ripped apart in my hands. Ethan stood behind me with his backpack slung over his shoulder. Spilled cereal crunched under my feet as I moved to the toaster and dropped my quarry in.

"I was only having a little fun," Ethan said. "I wasn't really going to call her, you know that, right?"

"It's not like we were dating then." I singed the tips of my fingers pulling the bagel from the toaster before the halves had popped. I stuck the wounded fingers in my mouth to cool them.

"Are we dating now?"

Ethan's question stopped me in my tracks. I pulled my fingers clear of my lips, wiping them on a napkin. Ethan and I had spent every minute we could together after we'd found the wall of wishes. After we'd shared a kiss, under the trees. My core tingled at the memory. I'd had a boyfriend back home and I'd put the brakes on things with Ethan until I could sort things out. It only seemed fair. We'd hung out as friends. But I'd looked after things at home over Christmas break. Things with Lucas hadn't been right for a while. Ethan was the one I wanted to be with. I thought it was what he wanted too.

Around us, there were shouts of reunion everywhere, scraping across my eardrums. The first time Ethan and I had seen each other since we'd been back at St. Augustus was in the foyer, with Courtney.

"I ended things with Lucas." My hands hadn't stopped shaking since leaving the foyer. I told Ethan I was going to do it. I thought it was obvious that I had, even though I hadn't told him it was done.

The conversation I'd had with Lucas was still raw, grating against something inside me. He'd tried to convince me to give our relationship more time, to work on it with him. I'd almost caved. But he couldn't know what my time at St. Augustus had been like. What I'd been through with Ethan at my side. There was no going back. I wasn't the same person I'd been before.

My shared history with Lucas hadn't been enough to carry me through the darkest moments I'd ever experienced. The trust we'd built through our years as friends had crumbled like a house of cards once we'd been apart. Once I'd encountered the fountain.

"I'm sorry. I'm sure it was hard," Ethan said. "And I don't want to rush anything."

My heart raced. Had Ethan changed his mind? "Don't you want us to date?" I asked.

"Yes, of course," he said in a rush, taking my shaking plate from me.

"Okay, then." Was it as simple as that? I wasn't in a hurry to ramp things up between us. They were good the way they were. Really good. I didn't have much more to give. There was a lot on my mind. I followed Ethan down the aisle between the long tables in the cafeteria to our regular spot. He pulled out a chair for me and I eased myself into it.

"Look Ava, Courtney's *supposed* to be here. She's going to swim, just like before your wish. We can't reverse it all, although at least some of it will return to normal. We can return to normal."

We could go on with our lives. It's what he wanted. What I wanted too.

But it wasn't that simple. *Everything.* That's what the wish had changed. Absolutely everything. My dad had been an engineer before my wish. Now he ran a construction crew and lived with my Aunt Mia and Uncle Chuck instead of the home I'd grown up in. I sighed. We were stuck in a loop that replayed itself. It stretched all the way back to our parents.

"Do you ever think about my dad's wish?" I asked. "If he hadn't made my mom fall in love with him, maybe she would have married your dad."

"Then the two of us wouldn't exist." Ethan's words were uneven. "We wouldn't be here right now, having this conversation. But we do exist and we're here, starting the New Year together. Everything is as it should be." Frustration bubbled through his words. His lips were pulled into a serious line that was out of character for him.

I wasn't trying to be difficult. I was just sharing the bleakness running through my mind.

"Save the West Woods!" A screeching voice rattled through

the cafeteria, turning heads.

"What's the old bat want now?" Ethan muttered.

A wild-eyed Ms. Krick loomed over our table, waving a handful of pale blue sheets of paper. Her gray bun was pulled so tight her cheeks were taut. She pushed a bundle of them into my hands. SAVE THE WEST WOODS was printed in black across the top of first page. I flipped through the stack. They were all the same.

"We need every voice," Ms. Krick said. She wore a drab tweed skirt suit, her wrinkled white blouse tucked in at the waist. She was like a student, dressed up as Ms. Krick for Halloween with her every quirk exaggerated.

"Happy New Year, Ms. Krick." Ethan slipped into conversation with our least favorite teacher, who had been at St. Augustus so long our parents had her as a teacher. "Why do we need to save the West Woods?"

Krick was known for her maniacal focus on the school's history. Specifically, she was obsessed with the woods, though we were fairly certain she'd never found the fountain.

"They're putting in a highway and destroying it all." Ms. Krick's voice rose, as she whistled through her nose.

"A road?" My voice was quiet. A road was going through the woods? The blood drained from my face. The fountain was there.

"Don't the woods belong to the school?" Ethan asked, reaching for one of the flyers in my hands.

"Headmistress Valentine has overstepped her bounds this time." A ravine full of wrinkles appeared on Ms. Krick's forehead. "She's gone and sold the land. It's not her right to allow the interstate extension on the school's property." Her cheeks trembled with agitation.

"They can't," I whispered, letting the flyers I held drop. They fluttered across the table in a fan.

"I shouldn't need to tell the two of you how important the woods are to the school." Ms. Krick leaned over us so closely that I could see threads of white cat hair on the lapels of her blazer.

Ethan's dark eyes narrowed as he read over the flyer.

"If the woods are destroyed," Ms. Krick said, spitting her

words as she leaned in. I cringed as her spray hit my face. "All will be undone."

CHAPTER TWO

Ava

"If the fountain is invisible when the woods are bulldozed, maybe nothing will be undone," Ethan said as we crossed the frozen campus lawn toward the gleaming sports complex later that afternoon.

The path under our feet had been cleared of snow, but we stepped carefully to avoid patches of slippery ice. It was only our first day back on campus and already thoughts of the fountain overshadowed us.

"Maybe." I rubbed my hands together to stay warm. The New England cold ached through to my Californian bones. Tomorrow, I'd have to start wearing uniform kilts again, when I was barely warm enough in my thick sweatpants. We were grasping at straws. Joining forces with Ms. Krick was abhorrent. But the threat of the fountain being destroyed was enough to set our boundaries aside.

"Krick's always been crazy." Ethan held out his gloves to me and I slipped their warmth over my hands. "Maybe she's wrong about the road."

We headed to the meeting announced on her blue flyers. Whatever Krick knew about the West Woods being torn down, we had to know.

"How can the school be in debt?" This part of Krick's story nagged at me. The asphalt path we followed was well maintained.

The campus buildings were in good repair. Classes were full. Something didn't add up. "Can't they just raise our tuition fees?"

"I don't know." Ethan's strides stilted. "I hope Krick's plan to stop this is less off-the-wall than her." He stopped to pack a snowball in his bare hands, throwing it against a nearby tree. It splatted against the trunk, then fell to the ground, leaving a circle of wet snow on the tree's bark.

"You still have your wish," I said. My subconscious had come up with an answer. I stopped walking. "You can go to the fountain now, and wish the road wouldn't happen." I'd used my one wish each student was granted on the mysterious fountain. Ethan hadn't. The fountain still appeared to him when he went to the clearing by himself.

"I shouldn't need to. Bulldozers can't kill magic." He dried his reddened hands on his jeans. "Think about it. The fountain can't be that fragile. If the contractors aren't students, the fountain won't even show up. They can't destroy something that isn't there."

"What if it shows up when a student zooms down the interstate? Some of the seniors have cars. How is that better?" A chill ran up my spine at the thought of solid stone appearing in front of a moving car. I'd sat beside the fountain and run my hands along its solid basin. The damage it could do would be catastrophic.

Ethan scuffed at a skiff of snow just off the path with his runner. He was holding something back. There was something he wasn't saying.

"Just go to the fountain and wish the road doesn't get built," I repeated. "The fountain has the power to grant it." Maybe he hadn't understood what I meant.

He sucked a breath through his teeth, stuffing his hands in his pockets. "The fountain knows what's in your heart..." he trailed off. "What if it grants me something else? Something I didn't ask for?" His voice was quiet in the crisp air.

I wish for Ava. It had been on the wall with all the wishes ever made. Etched with light at the end of the list. And then it had disappeared.

"But you didn't make that wish," I whispered.

"Of course not." He spoke quickly. "I didn't say it out loud, yet the fountain knew what I was thinking anyway. The thought gives me the creeps. What if something else pops into my mind and the fountain grants that? I couldn't. I don't want to. I like things the way they are."

His voice shook. I'd never seen Ethan this way. He usually shrugged things off. Was he afraid of the fountain?

"You don't need to wish for me anymore," I said.

"Don't I?" Ethan asked. His playful tone was back, if jaded. It was the second time that day he'd questioned me about our relationship although his reaction to the fountain was more pressing. "You've been pretty distracted."

His words settled on my shoulders like a giant weight. Of course, he was right. We'd started our relationship with a giant cloud over our heads and I'd done nothing to disperse it.

"Don't get me wrong," Ethan said. "I'm not planning to make a wish, ever. I've seen what it's done to you and I want nothing to do with the fountain. There seems to always be a catch. And wishing about the road definitely isn't my deepest desire. The chances of it working are slim to none."

His deepest desire. What could be more important than our existence? "Preventing us from being wiped off the planet isn't your deepest desire?" He was missing the point, completely. This was bigger than his fear of the fountain. My hands were on my cheeks as though he'd slapped me, although there was a gaping distance between us.

"Ava, I just don't think I should add a hasty wish to the wall." His voice was full of emotion. "Look at you."

Wintry streaks of tears froze on my cheeks in the wind. Something inside me was broken and he was calling me out on it. He was right, of course. He usually was. My wish had all but destroyed me. I'd worked hard to piece my world back together, although I hadn't pulled myself together, yet. Maybe I never would, completely. Ethan put his arms around me. My core shivered a little less in his embrace.

"There you are!" Margaret called to us from the door to the

sports complex. Her arm was linked with a smiling Courtney. My pulse roared in my ears. How was I supposed to stay out of Courtney's path when the girl was *everywhere*?

"We have a new teammate." Margaret smiled, shoving Courtney ahead of her.

"Yes." I should have tried to hide my frown, but Courtney's presence pressed against me, sucking the air out of the sky. I wiped my tears with the back of the gloves Ethan had lent me. We went forward, hand in hand. I pasted a smile on my face. I could do this. We had to know if the road was real. If it was, we had to stop it.

At the front of the auxiliary gym, dozens of folding metal chairs were set up in rows.

"Ava and I have met," Courtney said. Her teeth shone like perfect pearls as she bobbed along beside Margaret. Yes, we'd met. My temples throbbed. I wasn't good at duplicity. We'd met dozens of times, if my dreams counted. Her smile was like a punch in my gut. I'd stolen her destiny and she was smiling at me, clueless. This secret had wormed its way into my consciousness but it wasn't buried. It might never be.

"Are we the only ones here?" Ethan's words echoed in the empty gym.

"Looks like it," Margaret said. "Ms. Krick will be here any minute, she's never late."

"We'll have to recruit," Courtney said, hands on her hips. "They can't knock down trees to build a road."

I bristled at her zeal. "Why are you helping?" My words slipped out before I could think. This Courtney had no connection to the school, to the woods. Nobody else had showed up to Ms. Krick's call to action. Why was she here?

Courtney's green eyes sparkled with life. Nothing about them reminded me of the calculating girl I'd wished away. I couldn't reconcile the two. Maybe she was just a really good actress. I averted my eyes. Courtney had made my life hell. How could I let that go? I shifted my weight from foot to foot. My heart hadn't forgiven her. It didn't know how.

"I invited her," Margaret said, stepping between us.

"Ava really loves the woods," Ethan said, his tone apologetic. "Her gran lives on the other side."

His words were a cue for me to get myself together. Heat throbbed at the nape of my neck. I didn't want him to speak for me, even if I couldn't form the words myself.

"What does your gran say about the road?" Margaret asked.

"I-I…" I stuttered. I hadn't thought about Gran at all. She could be stuck living beside a highway. Or worse, she could lose her home.

Ethan put his hands on my shoulders and steered me toward the gray chairs before I could say anything more. The cold metal of the seat seeped through my sweat pants. It did nothing to quell my shaking.

"Give Courtney a break," Ethan said, in a low voice. "She doesn't even remember you."

I had to get a grip.

"How could the school be in debt, is that even allowed?" asked Margaret, as she took the seat beside me. "St. Augustus has been here for almost a hundred years."

I stared at the empty stage and sat on my gloved hands. Nothing good would come of me answering Margaret. It was best if I stayed silent.

"See?" said Ethan, gesturing to the back of the gym, where Ms. Krick shuffled her way across the floor to the front. "Ms. Krick is here. We'll find out what's going on." He put a hand on my knee.

Ethan, Margaret, Courtney and I sat in the folding chairs. Thankfully Margaret was between Courtney and me.

Krick clapped her hands three times. The sound reverberated from the gym walls and metal-beamed ceiling. She faced us with her hands on her hips. She still wore the threadbare skirt suit she'd had on in the cafeteria, but her blouse was puffed out, as if she had a sweater on under it.

"Find yourselves a seat." Her shrill command was unnecessary. Only the four of us were there and we were already seated. If Krick was surprised at the low turnout, she didn't let on. "Headmistress Valentine will tell you that St. Augustus has been experiencing financial issues." She launched into her teacher lecture voice while pacing at the front of the gym.

"Can you tell us how much debt the school is in?" Courtney called out.

I stared at Courtney. Of course, I'd wondered the same thing, but blurting it out in the first minute was bold.

"This administration has been running at a deficit for years." Krick's eyes darted to the gym doors, as though Valentine would overhear her. She pulled at her skirt. Her twitchy hand patted at the bun in her hair. "There have been many cutbacks in amenities this year. Have you noticed?"

Her piercing eyes chilled me. What were we supposed to notice?

Ethan shrugged, catching my eye. He didn't know what she was talking about either.

"First, they changed the brand of coffee in the teachers' lounge." Ms. Krick threw her hands into the air. "Then it was delaying repairs on the teachers' residence. We've lost three teachers in the past five years. None of them have been replaced."

I shifted in my seat. There was no way for us to know what coffee brand was served in the teachers' lounge. Or what was being repaired in the apartment she held in the teachers' residence. Ms. Krick was ranting. I'd seen it before, but it still unnerved me when she embarrassed herself. What did this have to do with keeping bulldozers away from the fountain?

"St. Augustus enrollment was down again this year." Ms. Krick was getting warmed up. Her voice rose to a pitchy yell. "They're even allowing students to waltz in mid-year to compensate." She wagged a finger at Courtney.

"Our families pay tuition," said Courtney. "Isn't that enough?"

I winced as Ms. Krick threw her hands in the air.

"It isn't even enough to cover the taxes." Ms. Krick shook her head so vigorously the loose skin under her chin quivered. She'd worked herself into a fever. "Isaac Young built this school for you, the students. The West Woods is an integral part of your school experience."

The hair on the back of my neck prickled at the mention of Isaac Young. He was one of Ms. Krick's obsessions, and from what we'd learned, he built the fountain. He'd given it power.

"Don't schools get breaks on taxes?" Ethan asked.

I crossed my arms. I didn't care about taxes. I was hyper-focused on the woods and so far, we hadn't learned anything helpful.

"The town of Evergreen has been after the West Woods for a decade." Ms. Krick's voice dipped as though she were telling us a ghost story. "It's been quite the tussle. Three years ago, City Hall had St. Augustus' property reassessed, at several times its true market value. The property taxes imposed were crippling to the school. Valentine fought it, of course, but she lost. Selling the West Woods is her peace offering to them. A white flag."

Krick's pacing strides were long, four in each direction before turning to walk the other way in front of the stage.

I was no stranger to Krick's long-winded speeches, although this one had more substance than her usual ravings. She was quoting real facts, if they were true. Did the town really want the road to go through the woods? Or was there more to it?

"The back pay is due this year. It's a sizeable amount," Krick continued. "The school's lawyers proposed the land trade. It clears the back-taxes for the school and leaves a cushion for future payments."

My mouth went dry. This meeting was pointless. We were too late. It was a done deal.

"How does that help the school long-term?" Ethan asked. "It'll only balance the budget for a few years. It sounds like a band aid solution."

"That's right." Ms. Krick pointed enthusiastically toward the ceiling. Her triumph was out of place. Did she only want to embarrass Valentine's administration?

"Let's get out of here," I mumbled to Ethan.

His hand was still on my leg. He squeezed my knee gently, asking me to stay.

Ms. Krick spoke in half-truths at the best of times. If the problem originated with Headmistress Valentine's office, we'd get more answers there.

"Matilda, what are you going on about?" A voice came from

behind us.

The four of us swiveled in our seats to see Headmistress Valentine. Her tidy flat shoes tapped across the wood floor as she made her way to our measly gathering.

"Everything has been sorted, there's nothing for these students to worry about. These are problems for our administration to handle, not for children to fret over," said the Headmistress.

A moment earlier, I'd thought we'd get straight answers by going to Valentine. But one look at her stony expression made me think twice. Valentine towered nearly a foot over Ms. Krick, who visibly shrank in her shadow.

"You can't just sell the woods," I said, my voice low as I got to my feet. "There must be another way."

Valentine wasn't denying there was going to be a road. So, it was true. Ethan rose to stand next to me.

"You've got them all worked up," Headmistress Valentine scolded Ms. Krick. She then turned to face me. "Ms. Marshall, new roads are built every day across the country. The school still has plenty of land for expansion of our buildings without the woods. By the time you students graduate, the road will be built and life will go on. We'll have forgotten this nonsense."

Or I would never graduate, instead suspended in some reality that never came to pass. My head spun. The fountain had linked my parents together, made their bond unbreakable. It had made me. If it disappeared, I could too, replaced by whatever alternate world my father had erased with his wish.

"Tell her," Ms. Krick said. Her gray eyes flared at me.

My pulse quickened. What did she want me to tell Valentine? Time slowed in the gym. Did Ms. Krick know about our wishes? My dad's? My head swam with confusion.

"What's that?" Courtney asked, getting to her feet and pointing.

We all looked up to follow her gaze. Margaret squealed as a flurry of brown feathers sailed through an open window high up in the gym wall. An owl's wide wingspan spiraled down toward us, casting a shadow on our gathering.

CHAPTER THREE

Ava

"Eep!" Margaret squealed again as she threw herself onto the gym floor at my feet, covering her head with her arms. Folding chairs all around us toppled to the ground with a deafening clatter, including the one I'd been sitting on moments before.

"Matilda, control that bird," Headmistress Valentine said through clenched teeth. She shielded her eyes, following the owl's swooping circles around the metal beams that criss-crossed the ceiling of the gym.

I'd grabbed onto Ethan's arm in the commotion. My heart raced. I'd seen that owl before, in the treetops of the West Woods.

"Shoo!" said the Headmistress as she waved her hands at the owl, which paid her no mind.

"He's not going to hurt anyone," said Ms. Krick, lifting an arm to stop Valentine's wild hand motions. "It's okay, Izzy. You can come down."

The owl dipped one wing at an angle then came to rest on the stage behind Ms. Krick.

"This meeting is adjourned," Headmistress Valentine said to us. "You may go."

I stood frozen and none of the others moved either.

"Did she just call the owl *Izzy*?" Ethan asked me in a low voice.

"No, no," Krick said. "He's come to lend his voice. The woods are his home."

A titter came from the entrance to the gym, where a handful of students had gathered, drawn by the commotion.

"Come in, come in," Ms. Krick called to the doorway. She waved her arms for the newcomers to join us. None did but Ms. Krick still beamed. "I'm glad you're here too, Moira, as I unveil my plan to save the West Woods," she said to Headmistress Valentine.

Ms. Krick shrugged off her ill-fitting blazer, hanging it with neat corners over a nearby chair. My mouth hung agape as she began to unbutton her blouse with her knurled hands.

"What's she doing?" I whispered to Ethan.

"She's having a complete meltdown," Ethan said out of the side of his mouth. "This is hard to watch."

"We should stop her," Margaret said, tugging on the hem of my hoodie.

Her horror crept along the bones of my arms, mingling with my own. Ms. Krick was a runaway train and I wasn't about to step in front of it and get crushed.

"Matilda, stop this right now." Headmistress Valentine rushed to grab Ms. Krick's blazer, throwing it over her. When Ms. Krick batted it down, Valentine grabbed at Krick's blouse, holding it together at the top. But Krick already had three buttons undone and pulled her blouse over her head, discarding it with a flourish. It sailed through the air, landing in a heap on the stage, where the owl perched, his spindly talons gripped along the edge.

I let out a long breath, feeling a gurgle of relief in my throat to see Ms. Krick wore something more substantial than undergarments under her blouse.

"Stop this striptease, right now," said Valentine, using her best principal voice. But Ms. Krick wasn't done. She undid her skirt with a swish of her hand, letting it drop to the floor.

The catcalls from the doorway fell quiet. The gym was as silent as death. I could almost hear the owl's eyelids blink over his beady yellow eyes.

Ms. Krick held her thin arms out to her meagre audience, as if she were atop an Olympic podium. My relief turned into a giggle. I covered my mouth and faked a cough. Ms. Krick stood before us dressed in an ice-blue skating costume, complete with a very short skirt that barely covered her crotch and sequins sewn in waves across the bodice. Her bare knees sagged with scandalously baggy skin. The shine from her bodice cast an effervescent hue across her face.

"Matilda, you get dressed right now!" Headmistress Valentine ordered, scampering to pick up Krick's discarded clothes.

The back of the gymnasium rocked with laughter. The four of us clumped together at the front exchanged bewildered glances.

None of this phased Ms. Krick. She pulled at her bun, shaking her head until her gray hair was loose in a high ponytail, hanging crookedly off the side of her head. I covered my eyes with my hand. My senses were overloaded.

"She looks like she escaped from a music box," Ethan said, under his breath. "A geriatric one."

I peeked between my fingers. Ms. Krick was still there, in all her ridiculousness.

Margaret snapped a hand over her mouth.

"Way to go, Ms. Krick!" a boy in senior year yelled from the door. Scattered applause and laughter had erupted in full force behind us.

"We are going to have a winter carnival, to raise awareness and save the woods," Ms. Krick announced, twirling at a pace that threatened to crack her slight frame in two. Her skirt floated about her frail hips like a flower. Her cheeks pinked with excitement.

Headmistress Valentine stood with her arms full of Ms. Krick's crumpled clothes. Izzy the owl swiveled his head so that his amber glowing eyes were fixed on Ms. Krick, who commanded the stage.

"Now, who will help me sell tickets to the carnival?" Ms. Krick asked.

Ms. Krick's disrobing was all anyone could talk about at supper in the cafeteria that night.

"I can't believe you were there," my roommate, Jules, gushed. She blew her fringe of black bangs out of her eyes and flipped her mane of hair behind her shoulder. "Did she really take off her suit in front of you? I'm so mortified for her."

"It wasn't really all that exciting," I mumbled. Why was I defending Ms. Krick? I pushed my food around on my plate. There was no way I could eat. Even Ethan didn't have a quip to diffuse the gloom that had settled over the two of us. Ms. Krick was more interested in playing dress up than actually saving the woods, that much was clear. The idea of a winter carnival was laughable. It couldn't raise the kind of money it would take to reverse the plans for the road that were already in motion.

Still, the four of us at the meeting had been wrangled into joining the organizing committee before we left the gym. Or at least Krick appointed us, over Valentine's objections.

The carnival was going to be held at a park a few blocks from downtown Evergreen. Ms. Krick said there was a skating pond, hence her ludicrous outfit. Ethan had announced that he wouldn't wear a skating costume and then somehow, we were in charge of planning it.

"Are you really going to help Krick plan this carnival?" Jules asked. "There are so many better causes we could hold a carnival for. Like getting a space on campus for the clubs and teams to congregate." She'd been talking about needing more student space on campus since the fall. Given what we'd learned about the state of the school's finances, that wasn't going to happen.

"Who would go to a carnival?" Jules' boyfriend, Jake, asked, his question dripping with disdain. He ran a hand through his blond hair.

"Ava's gran lives on the other side of the woods," Ethan said. "We have to do what we can to stop the road." His words shook me out of the funk I'd been in. It was the second time he'd mentioned Gran and the second time I hadn't given her a second thought.

I cleared my throat. "We'll do what we can to stop it. There has to be a better place to build a highway."

Gran's house on the other side of the woods gave us some cover to throw ourselves into this cause without drawing too much attention to how zealous we might get. I couldn't imagine the eye rolls Jules would give us if we tried to explain our real interest in the woods. Magic was a tough pill to swallow and I wouldn't believe it myself, if it hadn't happened to me.

CHAPTER FOUR

Courtney

I was supposed to be at St. Augustus. My bones had told me that the minute I'd come across its ivy-covered buildings in an online search. After months of begging, my parents had finally agreed to let me attend.

"I don't see how it can be a reputable school, Courtney," Dad said. "I've never heard of it."

I giggled now at Dad's reluctance. He didn't know everything.

My assigned dorm room smelled of must and yellowed books and everything about it was perfect, even my roommate. Margaret's sleeping face was squished against her pillow. She breathed loudly through her mouth, which hung open. I'd been moving around our room for fifteen minutes and she hadn't stirred.

She and I had hit it off immediately when I'd arrived on campus the day before. It was like we'd known each other for years. She'd gushed about finally having some company, which calmed my nerves. At least she wasn't mad about having to share her room, which she'd had to herself before Christmas.

Margaret had taken me to a kooky West Woods meeting, which had been highly entertaining. I smiled as I thought of Ms. Krick, my new English teacher, making a fool of herself in her skating getup. I had to hand it to her though. She was putting herself out there, although I wasn't sure she was going to be a very good teacher. The other kids didn't think much of her.

The winter semester was starting that morning. If my other teachers had half the personality Ms. Krick had, there wouldn't be a dull moment. I was looking forward to every minute.

I picked up an armload of clothes Margaret had discarded on the floor, depositing them on top of her dresser. I dusted off my hands. When she woke up, maybe she'd get the hint. She'd had this room to herself before. She might need a little nudge to keep it tidy.

I pulled my bushy orange hair into a knot on top of my head, wincing as my bed creaked with my shifting weight where I sat.

I was the new girl, for the first time in my life, and the thought gave me butterflies, in a good way. My father had no sway here. I was freer at the school than I'd ever been in my life. Maybe I should have been scared, but I wasn't. I wanted to embrace every new experience that came my way.

Ava was a puzzle though. She was skittish around me. Maybe she was like that all the time, but I got the impression I'd offended her. I had no idea how. Whatever I'd done, I had the rest of the year to make amends. She'd come around. I could only be myself.

My narrow bed creaked again as I stood. Margaret flopped an arm over her head, her eyes staying closed.

Our room was sparse, with two beds, two desks and two dressers. My room in Boston had been a football field in comparison, although I wouldn't trade it. My sister Hanna had gone off to college in the fall and I'd been rattling around our house with only my parents to talk to ever since. I'd already laughed more since I'd arrived on the St. Augustus campus than I had at home in months. That had to be a good sign.

"Boarding school!" Mom had acted shocked, although I could almost hear the wheels turning in her head. With me gone, she wouldn't have to worry about how much time I spent without parental supervision, which was one of her favorite things to natter at me about. Most times, while Mom and Dad worked, I went on long runs through Boston's busiest streets, trying to beat my personal bests.

I squeezed my feet into my new cerulean blue running shoes. The sun wasn't up yet. I had hours to kill before my first class, but I couldn't sleep. It was the first day of my second semester of eleventh grade. Friendships at this school were already formed, teams already chosen for the year. I was leaving behind my athletic progress at my school in Boston, which wasn't much. Coach Laurel had given me hope that I might get to swim in a few meets this year. After talking with Ava, I wasn't so sure. I'd have to work on her some more. My stomach was a jumbled mess and a long run was just the thing to straighten me out.

I pulled on my new school hoodie, which sported a silver owl. I ran my fingers over the St. Augustus crest, remembering Ms. Krick calling the owl in the gym by the name Izzy. Was he the school's mascot? I smiled. Ms. Krick was like a mascot too, like a character out of a bad late-night comedy on television. It was going to be difficult to take English class seriously with her at the helm. Luckily English was one of my better subjects.

The ancient wooden door creaked as I slipped out of the room and into the deserted hall. My lungs filled with the dull winter air as I stepped outside. January mornings were as dreary here as they were in Boston, but my runs in the city were restricted to daylight hours. Even in my mature neighborhood, with its turn of the century houses set back from the tree-lined road, crime was ever present. Evergreen was small and the crime rate was low. It was one of the things that had convinced Dad to let me come.

My breaths puffed in a cloud as I lunged into a stretch. My hamstrings relaxed into the pose. It had snowed overnight. A path had been shoveled from the dorm steps and I stayed on it as I started to jog, falling into my natural gait. The soles of my new shoes sang in tune with the upbeat running playlist pulsing through my earbuds as my feet pushed against the pavement.

When I got to the sidewalk beside the road, I chose left. Right led to the town's center, where Dad and I had driven around the day before. I didn't know what was to the left, but adventure awaited. One day soon, I'd know all the roads around the school.

Margaret had pointed out the West Woods the previous day.

They were the woods Ms. Krick's carnival was supposed to save. How could anyone argue with wanting to save trees? Planning a carnival seemed like a good way to meet people and Margaret wanted to be on the organizing committee. It was going to be fun, even if Ms. Krick had little hope of getting the attention she wanted. At least not the kind of attention that would help her cause. I smirked at the thought of her skating costume.

The West Woods flanked the school to the south and west. Its winter branches stood naked in all their glory, tangling its treetops together in rigid towers. I shivered as I passed, as though the forest had sucked all the warmth from my path and could pull me in. If the road wasn't so well lit, I might have turned back. Instead, I kept one eye on the trees as I stayed my course, watching shadows flicker between their branches.

"You're imagining the movement," I told myself, quickening my pace. I turned off my music and heightened my awareness of my surroundings, as I'd been taught to do when running alone. The only sound was a breeze whistling through the tops of the branches. I tried not to think of horror movies I'd seen, where the unsuspecting girl is grabbed in the woods. Horror movies gave me the creeps, but Hanna loved them and watched them when she used to babysit me, usually at some ungodly hour of the night when we were supposed to be in bed.

I pushed the wild thoughts from my mind as I ran. I was being ridiculous. This was Evergreen, not the backwoods those movies took place in.

My watch said I ran more slowly than my usual pace. Was it the cold? I frowned at the numbers on my wrist, slowing to a walk just as a loud crash came from within the nearby woods. I froze in place. A crack of branches splintering sent the hair on my arms into high alert. A warm bundle of fur hit me before I had time to scream, knocking me down with an unceremonious thud.

I was pinned to the ground by an immense weight, my mind reeling. My right elbow smarted from where it had struck the pavement and the breath was knocked from my lungs. A warm, wet tongue covered my exposed skin with its slobber. I spat thick fur out of my mouth. Mustering all my strength, I pushed the creature off me with two hands and rolled away onto my side, grunting with the effort.

My pulse raced. A large, white and gray husky dog frisked around me, still showering me with kisses. His front paws pushed at my shoulders.

"I'm so sorry!" The boy who jogged toward me on the path had a mop of hair as orange as my own hanging to his chin. It glowed unnaturally under the streetlamp.

"This is really unlike Husk. He must like you. I hope you're not hurt?" The boy tucked his unruly hair behind an ear and grabbed the dog by his leash, tugging mightily.

I blinked to get my bearings. It had all happened so fast. Husk's whiskery fur nuzzled against me, straining against the boy's grasp, melting whatever tension had built in my shoulders. He'd jumped on me with fervor only moments before, but now he was docile, climbing into my lap and snuggling in, spilling over the sides with his long limbs.

"He thinks he's a much smaller dog than he is," said the boy.

I laughed. Husk frisked his oversized body around me like a puppy. My elbow still hurt, but I was otherwise in one piece. I scratched Husk behind one ear.

"Come on, Husk." The boy tugged again, with little effect. Husk still sat planted firmly on my legs, his tongue hanging out in a pant.

"I'm Cole." The boy's smile stretched wide.

I reached up to pat my hair, which was halfway out of its messy bun. "C-Courtney," I stammered. Putting my back into the movement, I managed to shove Husk from my lap and scramble to my feet before he could reinstall himself.

"Are you hurt?" Cole asked, wrenching at Husk's collar. Husk had wrapped himself around my leg.

Heat crept into my cheeks as Husk buried his nose, embarrassingly, in my crotch. I guided his nuzzling away, as a wave of déjà vu crept up my spine.

What was familiar about this moment? I'd never been there before and I hadn't ever met Cole or his overly friendly dog. Cole's gaze was unnerving. In other circumstances, I'd probably never be able to bring myself to talk to him. But Husk had broken the ice.

"What's gotten into you, boy?" Cole scolded Husk, patting the dog's hind legs with a firm gesture. Husk obliged him by sitting. "Let me make it up to you?" Cole smiled at me in a disarming way.

I was almost afraid to ask what he meant. If I didn't know better, I'd think he was flirting with me, although I didn't have much experience with that. We'd met with me flat on the pavement and I'd since realized my elbow was bleeding, leaving a hot, sticky stain soaking through my hoodie.

"I'm fine, really," I said.

"Is that blood?" asked Cole, stretching for my elbow. His touch sent a tingle through me, even through my sleeve.

"It's nothing," I said, moving my arm away. "Just a little scrape."

My head felt woozy, although I couldn't tell if it was because he was standing so near or because of my fall. Something about this whole moment, about him, felt oddly familiar and I couldn't shake the tinge of regret it invoked.

"Have we met?" I finally managed to say.

The day before I'd met Ethan, who I'd spoken to in Boston in the fall. That had been a huge coincidence. Had I met Cole before too?

"Maybe we've seen each other in town?" he offered, cocking his head to one side.

My stomach sank a little. My gut screamed that I knew him, yet we couldn't have met in town. I'd only driven through there once with my dad the day before. "I-I just moved here this week. I must be mistaken."

I hadn't slept much. My memory must be playing tricks on me.

His nose was spattered with freckles, so like my own. Maybe our similarities were all I found familiar, like some long-lost relative. But I hoped he wasn't my relative. The flutter in my stomach would be very out of place if he were a cousin. Maybe I'd seen him on TV, but nothing about his untied shoelaces or the smudge of mud on his jeans reminded me of someone famous I should recognize.

"I know we just met, but Husk is a really good judge of character and he's smitten with you." Cole's smile was contagious. I let it infect me, spreading a smile across my face. "Since you're new to St. Augustus, allow me to show you around the town? We can get some pizza."

Husk rose from where he was sitting, wagging his tail as he nuzzling my knee.

"How do you know I go to St. Augustus?" The hairs on the back of my neck stood up. Maybe I was right about us meeting before and he'd been pulling my leg.

"Your hoodie," he said, stuttering a bit as he pointed at the school's crest. "Sorry, I didn't think that through before it came out of my mouth. I'm not a creep or anything. I'm… I'm not very good at talking to pretty girls, as you can see."

Blood rushed to my ears. His awkward speech was endearing. He'd called me pretty. Had he asked me on a date? Had he meant to?

"Pizza from Luigi's?" The name of the restaurant popped out of my mouth like I'd been there a hundred times. My stomach quivered. Was there a place called that in Evergreen? I absently patted Husk, who busily wove himself between my legs.

"Luigi's, sure. Tomorrow night," said Cole. "I'll leave Husk at home."

I must have seen a place called Luigi's when Dad and I drove around the town. Its neon red sign and checkered awning had popped into my head without prompting. Cole seemed to think it was a good place for pizza, so at least I hadn't embarrassed myself. I untangled my legs from Husk's leash, stepping over it a few times to unwind his web.

"You don't have to leave him at home," I said, scratching Husk behind his ear. He was so full of personality.

"I don't think he likes pizza," Cole said, laughing.

"Where do you go to school?" My question popped between us like an abrupt cloudburst. Students weren't allowed to have dogs in the dorm, he must live in town. I'd just said I would go on a date with a boy I just met, like girls in Hanna's horror movies always did. What if Cole were older than he looked? Or worse, younger. My hands stilled in Husk's fur.

"My family lives in town," he said, in a rush. "I go to Evergreen High. Eleventh grade."

My shoulders relaxed. He was my age. None of my fears were justified, yet my heart still pounded. This was a new year, a new school, a new beginning. Maybe this was just what I needed, to say yes to something that was out of my comfort zone.

"I do want to," I blurted, then clapped a hand over my mouth. My voice was too loud in the early morning air. I sounded like an idiot.

"Great," he replied then held something out to me.

"Uh..." I stared at the phone in his hand.

"For you to put in your number," he explained.

"Right," I said, recovering. I took it from him and tapped in my phone number. Husk ambled beside my hip, tugging at my jacket with his teeth. He looked up at me with unmatched eyes – one brown, one blue. He then let the hem of my slobber-soaked jacket drop, bolting for the woods.

"Catch him!" Cole cried, leaping into action. "It can take hours to catch him in the woods if he gets away. I have to get home before school."

I grabbed onto the leash flying behind a galloping Husk, which snapped the distance between us taut. I lost control of my own motion as his momentum led me through the frozen underbrush, branches grabbing at me from all sides as I struggled to stay on my feet.

"Heel, Husk!" I called the words that would have worked on my own dog back home, but Husk barreled onward, dragging me deeper into the woods, my runners skidding and tripping on uneven roots and hardened snow.

"Let him go if you have to!" Cole's out of breath voice called from far behind.

The chilled air on my face was fresh and bright and I kept running. Husk hauled me past the trees into a clearing, where his prints blemished the blanket of undisturbed snow spread out in an oval field. This dog needed obedience training. I'd talk to Cole about that.

"Ack!" I yelled, too late, as Husk scurried under a clump of branches.

I tried to drop the leash, but I'd wrapped it around my hand and it dug into my flesh. I was dragged into the snow on my belly.

"Husk!" My cheek crushed into the icy ground as panic pushed up my throat. I tucked my chin to my chest and squeezed my eyes shut as the leather strap yanked me past spindly branches that scratched my skin.

I skidded to a stop on the hardened mud. "Oh, buddy," I groaned.

Husk's breath smelled of tuna. His panting was hot on my wrinkled nose.

"I'm so sorry!" Cole's voice came from the edge of the clearing.

Moments later his face appeared, framed by the thick branches his hands pried apart. He was out of breath.

"How did you get in?" He pushed at the boughs, which swayed and sprinkled fir needles and dusty snow onto my collar.

My core pressed to the dirt as I unraveled my throbbing hand from the leash. Cold seeped through my hoodie and running tights. I rested my cheek on the dirt, letting my eyes flutter shut. I didn't need Cole to get in here with me. I needed to get out.

"I'm fine," I said, forcing my eyes open.

If I was a sight to behold before, I was surely ten times worse after being dragged under the trees. Husk's steaming tongue hovered over me. He looked pleased with himself, sporting a human-like grin. My right shoulder was pinned under a low branch. I wriggled it free against the tree's needles, which poked through my hoodie. I was a mess.

"Give me your hand," said Cole.

I looked down at my hand, which was white from being wrapped in the leash strap and streaked with mud. Cole had wanted to go on a date with me. Would he still want to after this? Husk's rough tongue licked my cheek, dragging over my eye. A laugh rippled through me, shedding my embarrassment with it. Husk barked along with my hilarity as I pushed myself to a sitting position.

"Gotcha," I said, wrapping Husk into a bear hug and burying my face in his fur.

I edged us both further under the trees where it was more spacious, like a cave with an evergreen canopy.

"Are you hurt?" Cole asked, still poking around outside the barrier of branches, his eyes popping through the brush near my head. "I can't figure out how to get in there."

"Only my pride is hurt," I said. "Here. Pull Husk out. I'll crawl out the back way." I grabbed Husk's leash and shoved it through the Christmas tree backdrop. Cole relieved me of the leash and I took a moment to sit and compose myself before slumping down on all fours to go back the way I'd come. I leaned back, expecting to find the support of a tree trunk. Instead, something cold and solid pushed at my back. I twisted, frowning at a thick mess of criss-crossed branches. I scrabbled to move one aside, uncovering a low stone wall. I pulled out my phone and turned on the light.

"Do you need help?" Cole asked. "I can tie Husk up and come in. The branches are thinner over here, maybe you could get out." He'd moved around the trees to my right.

"I'm fine," I said. "I just need a minute to catch my breath."

"Okay." His voice wavered.

Words etched on the wall I'd uncovered danced in the shadow of my flashlight beam, each letter's edges worn with time.

"What is this?" I whispered.

The wall beckoned to me. I stretched out a bare finger. It was a list of sorts, with dates beside each entry.

"I wish..." I read the etched letters aloud. The moment my hand touched the cold stone, a jolt of electricity ran through my arm. I jerked my hand away as if the wall was on fire instead of ice cold. What had just happened? I squinted at the wall then tried again, this time placing both my palms flat against the rock. My spine stiffened as my connection to the wall was made. A hazy sensation overcame me.

"Courtney?"

I heard Cole's voice, but I'd been pulled into some kind of trance. He sounded far away. The wall came alive under my touch, glowing with a golden warmth that rippled through my core. The den around me filled with colored light, like a movie playing on a drive-in screen, images of people sharpening in front of my eyes. Their voices filled the space under the trees. My jaw dropped to my chest as my own likeness entered the scene I watched, wearing a hardened stare.

"Is that me?" I whispered. It *was* me, but from another timeline, one that came flooding back. My eyes widened as I watched my own likeness, walking with Cole. I'd met Cole before. I hadn't been wrong.

I held my breath, barely daring to blink. I didn't want to miss anything. This past was *my* past. I remembered it clearly now. I'd made a wish on a fountain in these very woods, just outside this stand of trees.

The past I'd somehow forgotten played out before me. The desperation I'd felt in those moments echoed through my bones. The things I'd done to Ava. How I'd treated Cole.

Scenes flashed before me with excruciating detail. The fountain had pushed me to my brink. It had broken me. It had taken every last piece of my decency with it. I pulled my hands off the wall. My breaths came in short rasps. I wanted it to stop.

"Courtney?" Cole called.

My world had changed in a moment. My mouth was dry. My past, my present, my wish, all of it smashed onto my shoulders like a pane of glass, breaking, splintering shards all over me.

Time jumbled up in my mind. I dropped my phone as my hands flew to my temples. There was no light under the trees now. I'd thrown a coin into a fountain and become the worst possible version of myself. And then I'd come back to the clearing, but the fountain wasn't there. I'd thrown another coin into the grass and begged for a second chance. This was my second chance. It had been granted.

"How?" I whispered.

Who I'd been and what I'd forgotten scratched itself across my mind like nails down a chalkboard. I'd been given a second chance. I wasn't so sure I deserved it.

The branches closed in around me where I sat under the trees. I'd made a wish. I'd wished to get everything on a list, a list of stupid stuff that would get me into college. And then it had been granted and I'd become someone else. Someone who would stop at nothing. Someone who *could* stop at nothing. Propelled by the magic of the fountain.

"Courtney?" Cole called.

I couldn't answer him. What would I even say?

My hands clawed at branches, tearing them down, snow and all. Their bark bit into the flesh of my mud-caked palms. Chunks of ice shook loose from the trees above, raining down onto my face, stinging my skin.

"There you are." Cole beamed at me as I emerged from under the trees. Husk frolicked next to him, chasing his tail.

"Did you hear all that?" I asked him, my heartbeat throbbing in my eardrums.

"I heard you tell those trees to get lost," he said and laughed, then paused. "Are you okay? You're really pale."

I was more than pale. I was going into shock. I recognized the symptoms from my first aid training at swimming. My hands shook. "I – I've got to go." I needed to get out of the cold.

"Okay," he said, his voice shaky. "So, tomorrow night?"

"Sounds good," I called over my shoulder as I jogged away, my legs trembling.

I had to get out of the clearing. Cole didn't remember me. He didn't know about the fountain or the secrets of the school. And I'd almost forgotten too. Almost.

"No wonder Ava hates me," I said to myself.

Brittle twigs grabbed at my hair, pulling it from its roots, but I didn't stop. Cole was going to think I was nuts. He would probably cancel our date. I needed to get out of the woods. A wall of branches blocked my way. I skidded to a stop, panting for breath.

If I'd been given a second chance, I was wasting it. I doubled over, placing my muddy hands on my knees. The fountain had controlled me once. I was free of it now. The new road was going to destroy the woods, along with the fountain, and not a moment too soon. It had caused me nothing but pain.

I remembered Ms. Krick's busybody nature. She was wrapped up in the magic of the school. Yes, the magic. I'd said it, if only inside my own head. There was more. I remembered now. I shuddered at the clarity my past provided. The carnival was bound to fail and that was okay, because the fountain had to go.

The edge of the woods was quiet, with no sign of Cole or Husk. An owl's call echoed through the treetops, sending a shiver up my back. Izzy. His eerie hoot shot through my chest. My soaked running shoes skidded on the hardened ice under me as I scrambled to accelerate. It was all too much. My feet caught on the ground and I burst through the branches ahead, letting the snow rain down on me. I was going to help the road get built. Then I'd always be free.

CHAPTER FIVE

Ava

"Ava, can you be civil?" Ethan asked, frowning.

I'd rambled on about the road so much our friends had drifted away one-by-one, leaving Ethan and me alone together in the crowded student lounge before the first day of classes. We'd eaten breakfast early, then gathered to talk more about our holidays. Except all I could talk about was the road.

Light snow fell outside and most of the student body milled about the lounge, visiting. It was like I was watching myself from a perch on the wall, as if someone else repeated the same phrases over and over. I didn't know how to stop. I couldn't let go.

"I don't think I can trust Courtney," I said.

I sat sideways on one of the dozens of brown leather armchairs in the lounge, my feet slung over its arms, my kilt carefully arranged so it didn't creep up. Ethan was in the chair next to me, stirring his cold hot chocolate with a spoon on the coffee table in front of us. He'd eaten the whipped cream off the top without offering me any. Courtney's face had filled my dreams the night before. Why would she fight for the West Woods, unless she knew what was in it? She'd just arrived. The woods meant nothing to her. She wasn't supposed to remember anything that happened before.

"She's a peach," Ethan said.

I grabbed the spoon out of his hand and licked the whipped

cream off.

He laughed, but his eyes remained serious. "And her dad might be able to make some noise at Krick's carnival," he said. "We need all the firepower we can get. I'm not keen on my existence being erased."

"I know what she's capable of and I think we should leave her out of it," I said, tossing his spoon on the coffee table.

"I told you, you fixed her. Your wish made her nice." His logic had a certain whimsy to it.

I sighed. His positivity was having the opposite effect on me.

"Courtney could really help us raise awareness," he argued. "There's not many kids or teachers even paying attention to the school's deal to sell the land. We need every voice. Can't you just let it go? We have to live in the present or we'll go in circles, wondering about what might have happened in a different plane of existence."

"Jules said she'd help, too. She's terrific at swaying public opinion." I chewed on the inside of my cheek. Courtney made my skin crawl. She was a constant reminder of a time I wasn't proud of, a time I'd rather forget.

"Yeah, if turning the carnival into a fashion show will stop the bulldozers, we're in luck," said Ethan.

I looked up in surprise at his tone. Had his brow been creased that way this whole time? I swung my legs around, sitting up. There were fewer students in the lounge than there had been only minutes before. We needed to get moving to class soon or we'd be late.

But the last thing I needed was for Ethan to give up on me too. "You're not wrong," I said.

Jules was a master party planner, but her idea when we told her about the carnival was to crown a king and queen of winter. She'd be intensely focused on flashy decorations and the latest music. Jules' touches would make sure people came and had a fabulous time, but she wouldn't be doing it to save the woods.

"I will give Courtney a chance," I said. I could make myself do that. I didn't like the chill Ethan was giving off. I was acting like a petulant child. It was written all over his face.

"You could at least try," he said. "If you really can't do it, we'll find another way."

"Okay." My arms crossed over my chest. I had to think of Courtney as an ally. Ethan was right. Her dad's connections might be able to help.

"Good, because here she comes," he said.

My stomach lurched as Courtney wove her way through the chairs, making a beeline for us. Her hair was wild, her face streaked with dirt.

"She looks like she's been mud wrestling," I said, under my breath. I pitied the poor soul that took Courtney on.

"Ava, *try*." Ethan's voice was a whine. He was done with my complaining.

I supressed a smirk.

"Have you made a decision?" asked Courtney, getting straight to her point. Except I wasn't sure what her point was. Did she know I didn't want to work with her on the carnival? She couldn't possibly know that. Dread prickled up my neck. My fists clenched.

"Can I swim at any meets this year?" Courtney was slightly out of breath, as if she'd run all the way up the curved stairs to the lounge. The orange curls on her head stuck out in odd directions. Where had she been?

"Yes, of course," I said, my fists unfurling.

My answer was out before I'd had the chance to think. Courtney was supposed to be on the swim team. It was my fault she wasn't. But if I let her swim, she'd have to replace someone. Margaret was the weakest swimmer on the team. If Courtney had tried out in the fall, Margaret wouldn't even be on the team. How was Margaret going to react? I stole a sideways glance at Ethan, who nodded his encouragement.

"Just let me talk to Margaret," I said.

Courtney's smile fell as she grasped my meaning. "I'd be replacing Margaret?" she asked.

"She'll be fine," I said. And she would be. She'd still get to go to meets with us as an alternate. Margaret didn't like the pressure of competing anyway. She might even be relieved.

Courtney shifted her weight from side to side. "I, uh – I think we got off on the wrong foot," she said.

The skin at my temples tingled. I didn't like the way she looked at me, as if she knew me. She wasn't supposed to know me. Ethan nudged me in the ribs, snapping me out of my stupor.

"Thank you for the chance to swim," Courtney said, bobbing her head in a shallow nod. "I won't let you down."

"Have you been outside?" Ethan said. It was his roundabout way of asking about her appearance. I'd been wondering the same thing. Courtney was dressed in trainers, leggings, and the same St. Augustus hoodie she'd worn the day before. It was smeared with dirt now so nothing about it was new anymore. Had she been rolling on the ground?

"I went for a run in the woods," Courtney said.

I drew in a breath at her mention of the woods.

"Rule breaking already." Ethan's face broke out into a wide smile. "A girl after my own heart."

I shot Ethan a withering look.

"What?" Courtney asked.

"Going into the woods," he replied. "They're off limits."

"R-right," she stammered. "Of course. Well, I was chasing a dog. I guess I'm a bit of a mess. I didn't really mean to go into the woods."

"The woods?" Ms. Krick stood behind Courtney, dressed in a basic gray suit with no trace of her skating costume or bulky layers underneath, only a plain white blouse with a creased collar. "Who was in the woods?"

"Nobody," Ethan said, smoothly. "We were just talking about saving the woods. We're not sure that a carnival's going to be enough." He leaned forward.

"It will generate awareness," Ms. Krick said. "But you're right, it's not enough. Which is why Courtney had the foresight to get her father involved."

"Nice work." Ethan clapped his hands in appreciation. Courtney's eyebrows shot up as though she'd just been told her dad was a small green alien.

"Yes, he called me first thing this morning." Ms. Krick hopped up and down in a little jig. Her arms undulated in an awkward hula motion. Whatever dance she was trying to do wasn't from this century. Her watch had charms hanging from it that shimmered as she danced. I hadn't noticed them before. As she shuffled from side-to-side, she caught her footing on the carpet and stumbled.

"Whoa, whoa." Ethan grabbed Ms. Krick by her wrist, keeping her upright.

I winced. Sometimes Ms. Krick's battle-axe personality made it easy to forget how old and frail she was. Her wrists were only half the size of mine. Ethan let go of her abruptly, shoving his hands in his pockets.

"Dad said it might be hard to reverse if the school has already signed the title away," Courtney said.

"Construction is notoriously slow," Ethan added.

"Not this time." Krick's lower lip stuck out.

"Don't they need an environmental study?" I asked. I'd banked on us having a few months to fight the road before we really had to worry. I'd picked up a few tidbits on construction over the holidays, being with my dad.

"It was fast tracked with a study done a few years ago," Ms. Krick said. "I spearheaded the committee to stop the subdivision they wanted to build then. I'll stop this too." She puffed up her chest.

"I know the West Woods hold certain… traditions, and history that need to be preserved for the sake of the school…" Courtney's voice wavered.

"We'll make the case the highway will be dangerous and noisy. Disruptive to our students," Ms. Krick said. "Not to mention it would go right past the football stadium. How are athletes supposed to play with exhaust fumes in the air? We won't need to talk about the school's history. There are plenty of other reasons to highlight."

The arguments she listed were good ones. The fact that she'd stopped construction there before helped me breathe a little easier.

"Anyway, Senator Wallis is going to make some noise and come speak at the carnival." Ms. Krick wore a smug smile. "This is really about political pressure. Let's see the Headmistress stand up to that. Thank you, Miss Wallis."

Shouts and laughter coming from a table halfway down the long expanse of the lounge made Ms. Krick turn her head.

"Excuse me." She shuffled away, toward the group, mostly seniors.

"There goes the fun police," Ethan muttered, watching her.

"Thanks for covering for me, about me being in the woods this morning," Courtney said, rubbing her hands together.

"Of course," Ethan said. "But even if she did find out, you could always play the new card. You just got here. You can't be expected to know the rules."

Ethan and Courtney stared each other down. I held my breath. He was testing her. A long moment passed, where neither of them moved. Then Courtney flinched and looked away.

"Well, thanks." Her eyes were downcast. "I'm going to go get cleaned up." Courtney turned and left with a small wave of her hand, winding her way back across the student lounge to the stairs.

"That was weird," Ethan said. "Who gets that dirty from being in the woods?"

But nothing about Courtney surprised me. I couldn't let down my guard. She'd gotten her dad involved in our cause and that was a good thing. Our carnival now had a speaker, one that could put the pressure on.

"There was something odd behind her eyes," Ethan said, confirming my suspicions. I'd seen it too.

"Do you think she's hiding something?" I wanted it to be simple. I wanted to believe she was innocent.

"She was lying about the woods," he said.

"Why would she lie about that?" The Courtney I remembered always had an angle.

"Not about being there." Ethan frowned. "I believe she was in the woods but I could swear she knew about them being off-limits."

"So?" I shrugged. It was a rule at the school. Anyone could have told her.

"Why would she lie about it?" he asked.

He had a point. I squinted at something he played with in his hand. It glinted under the fluorescent light of the lounge.

"What's that?" I asked.

His frown disappeared, replaced by a smirk.

"I couldn't help myself," he said. "Ms. Krick always wears a watch but today, I noticed this hanging from it. It was just there, ripe for the taking."

"You stole it from Ms. Krick?" My voice went up an octave. Then I laughed. Ethan's antics were harmless and his nerves were made of steel.

"I was drawn to it," he admitted. "I'll give it back. I just wanted to see what it was."

The cobalt blue stone sat in his palm, no bigger than a quarter. It had a linked silver chain looped through a hole bored into its polished edge.

"Is it a gem?" I asked, stretching my fingers out to touch it. If it was a gem, it could be valuable. Ms. Krick would notice it was gone.

"It was glowing when I first touched it," he said.

My eyes went wide.

"I probably shouldn't have taken it," he said. "I don't know what came over me."

"It glowed?" Had I heard him right?

I stretched to touch it. It was shiny, but glowing? It sat in his palm, quietly staring at me like an eye.

"Maybe I imagined it," he said.

Exactly what I was thinking. He closed his palm, tucking the stone into the pocket of his hoodie. "If it doesn't glow again by tomorrow, I'll give it back." He gave me a sheepish look. "I'll tell her I found it on the floor."

For the first time since coming back to school, I saw him. He'd been here the whole time, supporting me. And what had I given him?

His features softened.

"Can I take you on a date?"

He gave me a lopsided smile. Ethan didn't blush easily, yet a hint of pink crept across his jawline.

"A date?" It was like he'd read my doubts. How did he always manage to do that? "That sounds great."

"Luigi's, after school tomorrow."

He squeezed my hand and warmth shot up my arm. It was the first moment we'd shared since I'd been back that my mind was focused on him. Only him.

"It's a date," I said. My shoulders relaxed. I'd make a bigger effort. Senator Wallis was going to help us oppose the road. He was a pretty big gun to have in our arsenal. We had a fighting chance.

CHAPTER SIX

Ava

The next morning, sun streamed down onto another fresh blanket of snow that had fallen overnight. Ethan handed me a banana and yogurt on our way to class. My mind had been clear enough to sleep the night before and I'd slept right through my alarm.

"Thanks," I said, peeling the banana immediately.

I would have missed class if Jules hadn't come back to the room to grab her books after breakfast. Jules did most of her morning makeup routine in the restroom down the hall, so she didn't disturb me. I'd witnessed parts of it – a gazillion strokes of her brush through her long black ropes of hair, teasing her eyelashes with mascara with such delicate precision she didn't look like she wore makeup at all. I didn't see the point.

Besides, our room had become crowded over the holidays. Jules had inherited boxes of decorations to store for homecoming that the cheer team passed around from year to year. She was the favorite for captain next year and would be in charge of Homecoming. I was proud of her even though it made our already stuffed closet unbearable.

"I had a visitor last night," Ethan said.

"Hmm?" I tossed the banana peel into the compost section of the garbage can outside the West Building, where our first class of the morning was. We didn't get visitors often, let alone after curfew.

"Izzy," he said. "He was on my windowsill, tapping at the glass with his beak incessantly after lights out." He demonstrated by banging the fingertips of one hand against the palm of his other.

"The owl?" I laughed, dipping the plastic spoon he handed me into the cup of yogurt and taking most of it out with one scoop.

Ethan nodded.

"Did you let him in?" It seemed like a natural thing to ask. I shivered from the cold or maybe from the image of Izzy's golden eyes as I shoveled the scoop of yogurt into my mouth.

"No way. Marcus was there and started yelling at Izzy. I didn't think I could explain wanting to let him in," he said.

He hadn't shared anything about the fountain with Marcus to my knowledge. Students brushed past us on their way into the building.

"He tried to shoo Izzy away, but the bird didn't budge. He just blinked at me through the window pane, like this." Ethan's face was up in mine, as he blinked his eyes slowly. He looked eerily like Izzy when he did it.

"I closed the drapes and tried to sleep while he scratched at the glass," he continued. "He was still there this morning when I woke up. I think he stayed all night."

"Creepy," I said, tossing my empty yogurt cup into the recycling and the plastic spoon into the garbage.

"Izzy's not creepy," Ethan said, lowering his voice as we crossed the threshold to the West Building. "I kind of like him. Then he flew away into the woods."

We climbed the wide steps to Ms. Krick's classroom on the second floor, side by side.

"Don't you think that's weird?" he asked.

"Everything about this campus is weird," I said, as we entered the classroom. "I'm getting used to it."

Ethan put his bag on a desktop and swung himself into his seat like he always did.

"What is she doing?" he asked.

I squinted to the front of the room, where Ms. Krick opened and closed the drawers to her desk with frantic swings of her arms, tossing pens, staplers and more calculators than anyone would ever need onto her desk. Ms. Krick's lips moved quickly, mouthing something silently. Her head snapped up and her gaze bored through me. I stood beside Ethan's desk, frozen to the spot. Ms. Krick broke eye contact, sinking down on all fours.

"Did you drop something?" Courtney stood over our teacher, peering down onto the tiled floor, where Ms. Krick ran her hands back and forth as if she were swimming the breaststroke.

This time Krick's suit was a mustard yellow tweed straight out of the nineteen-eighties, with a pink blouse underneath.

"Did she lose a contact lens?" asked Jules, as she snapped her gum at my shoulder.

Every pair of eyes in the room was on Ms. Krick, who mumbled in loud grunts as she ran her fingers across the tiles.

"Can I help?" Courtney asked, pulling her kilt over her knees and crouching down low to search.

Ms. Krick straightened up, clearing her throat. She clapped her hands three times, shooing Courtney away. "I have misplaced an item," she confirmed, her voice formal. "I will put the search on hold until after our lesson."

She patted her head, where not a single hair was out of place. Her stare was enough to send the whole class to their places.

I was distracted by a movement at the window then drew in a sharp breath. On the branch of the tall oak beside the building sat Izzy, staring right at us.

"You see him, right?" Ethan asked, his voice dipping.

"Yes, of course," I said. Did he think Izzy was a figment of his imagination? Izzy hop-glided to the window sill. He blinked several times before tapping the glass with his beak in successive pings, just as Ethan had described he'd done at the dorm the night before.

I held my breath as Ms. Krick's black patent heels clicked across the floor to the window.

"Izzy, do you know where my stone is?" she cooed to the bird.

Ethan and I exchanged a look. Snickers erupted through the classroom as Ms. Krick shoved the wood-framed window open with her bony shoulder. An icy wind whipped through the room, dancing along my legs above my knee socks. Izzy put his wings out to his sides and flew into the room, making a beeline for Ethan's desk. I scraped my chair backward, standing to get out of the way of his wide span. The classroom was much too small for him to fly around with ease.

"It's okay," Ethan whispered. I couldn't tell if he was talking to Izzy or to me.

"Izzy, what is the meaning of this?" Ms. Krick crossed the floor quickly, staring the owl down. She spoke to him like she was scolding a child.

Izzy leaned in tight to Ethan, as if to give him a hug. Ethan's eyes grew as wide as silver dollars as he patted Izzy's back. Izzy fit his wings around Ethan until his upper body was obscured by feathers. I stood at the ready, unsure if I should pull the owl off.

Ethan didn't seem perturbed.

"Izzy!" Ms. Krick's shrill voice was more like a sharp command for a disobedient dog than a reaction to a wild animal flying in through the window.

Izzy made a sound like he was clearing his throat, then spun on his spindly claws, spreading his wings again and freeing Ethan from his smothering embrace. Ethan sputtered, protecting his face with his hands as Izzy's feathers grazed his cheeks. The owl jumped off the desk, flying with a jerky motion to the windowsill, where his talons clacked on the wooden sill for just a moment before he sailed into the winter day.

"You!" Ms. Krick wagged a finger in Ethan's face, which scrunched up as if he'd been hit with a pillow. "You have it."

"Have what, Ms. Krick?" I asked, stepping between them.

"What are you talking about?" Ethan asked, opening his eyes and squaring his shoulders.

My stomach dropped out from under me as realization set in. Ms. Krick was looking for the pendant Ethan had taken.

"This is weird behavior, even for Krick," Jake mumbled from the desk behind Ethan.

"Izzy would only come to you if you had it," Ms. Krick said, grabbing Ethan by the wrist.

"I have no earthly idea what you're talking about." Ethan

wrenched himself free of Krick's grasp. "The owl is your pet, or whatever. Can't you control it?"

Ms. Krick's face turned crimson.

"And I'm pretty sure you're not allowed to grab me like you just did," Ethan said, rubbing his wrist.

Ms. Krick stared at him for a long moment, then turned on her heel and marched toward the door. "Class dismissed," she said in a loud voice, slamming the door open and clicking her heels down the hall. "Izzy! Izzzzy!" Her calls echoed through the stairwell.

Jake let out a low whistle. "Wow," he said, as a stunned silence filled the classroom. "What did you take from her, Roth?"

Ethan didn't answer.

"She really wants that stone back," I said in a low voice.

"I can't very well give it back now," he said, laughing as he pulled the pendant out of his cardigan pocket. "Although I'm not keen on being made master of her feathered beast, it's an interesting turn of events."

Jake had lost interest in Ethan, turning to discuss with the others what they should do with the free class they'd just been given. The decibel level in the room rose well above what it should be, as kids packed their books into their bags and walked out in groups.

"When he - er – hugged me, Izzy gave me this." Ethan fished inside his pressed button-down St. Augustus shirt. "He put it down my shirt with his beak."

"Are you two coming?" Margaret asked from the doorway.

The room had cleared out, leaving only Ethan and me huddled together at his desk.

"We'll be right there," I said, forcing a smile.

Margaret shrugged, turning to walk away with Courtney. When we were alone, Ethan held out the folded piece of paper.

"What is it?" I asked.

I pinched the paper between my fingers. An owl, delivering notes like a carrier pigeon?

"It's a bit damp," he said, wiping his hand on his sweater.

"Izzzzyyy..." Ms. Krick's calls came from outside, below the classroom window. I strained to see down to the ground, where she scurried along the tree line, shaking branches as she passed and peering up into the treetops.

"We should get out of here," Ethan said. "Before she gets back and searches me for her rock."

I unfolded the paper, taking care not to rip its weathered edges. From here, I was going straight to the restroom to wash my hands. Did owls transmit disease like other birds and the bird flu? I held the yellowed page, pinched gingerly in my fingers. It was scrawled with slanted strokes of black ink. I'd seen the writing before.

"This handwriting," I said. I ran my hand along one of the long edges of the page. It had been torn from a book.

"Looks old," Ethan said. "What does it say?"

"It's a page from Isaac Young's journals," I said.

He probably recognized it, too. I ran my fingers over the ink. They were the same jagged letters we'd seen when we'd studied the St. Augustus founder's journals in the library. When we learned the fountain could only be used by students, and only once. There hadn't been any torn pages in the books we'd studied. This must be from another volume. It was an entry dated a decade after St. Augustus was opened. The journals in the library had all been earlier, written about the time St. Augustus was built.

December, 1942

My wishing fountain's powers are greater than I thought and students' wishes more careless. The danger I've created keeps me up at night, yet I can't simply destroy it. If I do, everything that's been wished so far... all will be undone. Its powers must be bound.

His message sent a chill rippling through me. "All will be undone," I repeated the words. "Those are the same words Ms. Krick used." My voice a shadow of what it had been, moments before.

"So, it's true. If the fountain is destroyed..." Ethan trailed off, the color drained from his cheeks.

"Isaac Young was planning to bind the fountain's powers," I

said. But he couldn't have done it. If he'd succeeded, the fountain couldn't have granted our wishes, or Dad's, for that matter. "I was hoping we were wrong about all the wishes being reversed." Having it confirmed somehow made our predicament worse.

"Did he fail?" Ethan folded the note, lost in thought. "Wait, when did Isaac Young die?"

A wave of ice passed over me as I remembered what we'd learned. "December, 1942," I said. Isaac Young died shortly after writing this entry. Whatever he'd planned, he didn't have time to complete.

CHAPTER SEVEN

Courtney

Ms. Krick called an emergency meeting of the carnival planning committee later that same day. Her classroom was packed with cheerleaders and football players Jules had recruited to help with the carnival, which was quickly becoming Jules' own personal party. I'd been put in charge of the speeches, due to Dad being the headliner. I was supposed to spearhead our lobbying of Evergreen's City Hall, and get the message for the West Woods out to anyone who would listen from the city, the state, the world. This role suited me fine, although I didn't plan to put much effort into it. Ms. Krick was late, which was unusual.

"I can't believe you guys got a free period instead of English class this morning," Marcus said, his brown skin crinkling at the edges of his smile.

"We're making up for it now," Jake grumbled. "After school meetings are like having detention."

"Is it me or is Ms. Krick losing her marbles more than usual?" Jules asked, while doodling two crowns with a purple marker on the whiteboard at the front of the room.

I sat at a desk in the front row, drumming my fingers against the desktop. Yesterday, these kids had all been new to me, but my memories had returned. I'd known them since the ninth grade and they conversed with their predictable banter, although I wasn't included in their chatter. I was new here, as far as they knew. I hugged my arms to my chest. This day couldn't end soon enough for me. I needed to sleep, to let my dreams make sense of everything spinning in my head.

Ava whispered something to Ethan, then looked my way. I cast my eyes down, picking at the cover of the notebook I'd brought. My stomach churned. I'd have to keep a low profile. What I couldn't figure out was Ava. Every time she spoke to me, her hatred was clear and I couldn't blame her, considering how I'd treated her.

But something about this whole situation didn't fit. How was it that she knew what had happened before I'd been given my second chance? Had she been to the wall under the trees? Had she touched it?

A pang shot across my chest. Everyone here was trying to save the woods. To save the fountain, if they knew about it. It was hard to say if any of these kids had found it and whether they'd made wishes too.

I was going to be working against them. I touched my forehead, imagining *traitor* printed across it. Were my lies what Ava and Ethan whispered about? I closed my eyes, taking a deep breath. The pang in my chest had become a throb. A layer of guilt wrapped around me. I wasn't good at harboring secrets. I couldn't let this secret control me. If the road went through, the fountain would be destroyed. And when everything was erased, their memories of this time would be erased as well. They'd thank me if they knew.

The soft click of Ms. Krick closing the classroom door alerted me to her arrival. Kids clambered to find seats. Ms. Krick's face was a drab mask, with no sign of her earlier outburst.

"I've been informed that my participation in organizing the carnival is in direct violation of my contract with the school," said Ms. Krick, her lips pinched and her shoulders sagging as she made this announcement. "However, I am confident that this group of students will do what's right and the carnival will go on. I will lend you my support if needed, even though I have been forbidden by the powers that be to lead this event."

She stood at the front of the room for a moment, resting her steel gray eyes on Ava, on Jules, on me.

"You each know what needs to be done." Her words sent a shock wave through me. How could she be counting on me? She was placing her trust in the wrong hands. My stomach twisted as she left the room. She'd given up. The road through the woods would go forward. The past I'd seen would never come to be. And neither would this moment. It would all be erased. Ms. Krick closed the door behind her.

"Great, so we don't have to have a carnival?" Jake said, as he stood. "Let's go."

"This sucks," Jules whined, standing and slinging her book bag over her shoulder. "I would have been the best carnival queen."

"Wait!" Ava scrambled to the front of the classroom, waving her hands, her cheeks flushed. "Can't you see what's happening? Valentine won't let Krick speak because she might be able to stop the highway from being built in our backyard. Construction is slated to start this spring. There will be dust, and noise, and they'll ruin the campus."

Ethan joined her at the front of the room, standing at her side. His gray uniform pants were pressed impeccably, as usual.

"Valentine wants to silence us all," he said. His voice had an air of desperation. I sat up in my seat. I was missing something. "She doesn't think we can do it. But do we want to wake up to a pile of dirt and Mack trucks rumbling through our campus?"

There was a low grumble from the kids in the room.

"We can run this carnival without Krick," Ava said. "And save our campus in the process."

Ethan pumped his fist.

"I think a winter carnival's a great idea, no matter the cause," Jules added, as she joined them at the front.

Margaret stood and hurried to stand with them. "We don't need Krick," she said. "We can meet without her. We'll probably get a lot more done."

"Can there at least be pizza involved?" Jake asked. "I'm starving."

"Sure," Ava said. "Let's move this meeting to Luigi's."

Finally, the room erupted in raucous approval, chairs scraping the floor as kids got to their feet. I hung back as the others stampeded to the door. I didn't have to go. I'd asked my dad to speak at the carnival before I'd touched the wall. I'd wanted to help. I had to think of a plausible reason to ask him not to come. Staying close to the carnival planning was my best option to making sure it didn't succeed.

I followed the group down the wooden stairs out onto the lawn, which smelled of moist, sweet winter. In a few months, that would be replaced by the smell of a freshly tarred road.

"So now the real planning starts, right?" Jules laughed. "Without *her*."

My stomach flip-flopped as I thought for a moment that she meant me, but when nobody turned my way, I realized she meant Ms. Krick.

"Can't we just eat pizza?" Marcus groaned.

"You can eat pizza," Ava said. "Also cotton candy and corn dogs, when we pull this carnival off."

She and Ethan held hands, swinging as they walked. We were about a dozen crossing the lawn. The others chatted excitedly about their hopes for the carnival as we crossed the frozen grass.

I wrapped my jacket around my shoulders against the wind and doubled my pace to keep up.

"Do you think your dad can stop the road?" Ava asked, as she dropped back to talk to me when we hit the sidewalk that led to town.

I was still in my kilt, like many of the girls, and the skin on my bare legs bristled with every step.

"I-I don't know. My dad said he'd try." It was a truthful answer. Tomorrow I'd call him to cancel.

Our group headed straight for the checkered awning of Luigi's. It looked exactly as it had been in my mind when I'd suggested it to Cole. I stopped in my tracks. *Cole.* I pulled out my phone and saw two missed calls from an unknown number. *Crap.* The red dot that said I had a message waiting wasn't there. I hit dial on the number listed and it went straight to voicemail, an automated one rather than a personalized greeting. I couldn't be sure it had been him.

"Hi Cole," I said into the phone. "I see I've missed your calls. I'm headed into a meeting now, but I'd like to get together later. Let me know what time works."

"Are you coming?" Jules called to me from the top of the steps. "We're getting a table."

"Be right there," I said, smiling at her.

She disappeared back into the restaurant. I climbed the steps as the aroma of fresh baked crust made my stomach curl. The restaurant was dark and cozy, with neon lights announcing beer brands around the crown moulding on the ceiling. I'd been here many times before, in a different life. Marcus waved to me from deep within the restaurant. They'd seated our group at a long table near the back.

"Courtney," said a voice from behind me.

I spun around to come face to face with Cole. He was wearing jeans and a fresh white hoodie with a navy stripe across the front.

"Hi!" My voice was too bright. Too chipper. I'd completely forgotten our date until I'd seen the neon lights. It was all I could do to stop myself from slapping my forehead. "I called you back."

"Oh? I wasn't sure you'd gotten my messages." He shuffled awkwardly. "Have you asked the hostess for a table yet?"

"Now?" I asked. I hadn't even changed from school. A kilt and cardigan was the last thing I'd choose to wear on a date. Not that I'd ever been on one.

"Courtney, over here!" Jules headed toward us. She waved both arms over her head to get my attention.

"I-there's a meeting..." I said, gesturing to the group at the back. "You and I can sit somewhere else."

My insides writhed. I was screwing this up, just like I had before.

"Sorry," Cole said, taking a step back. "We can just do this another time if you're busy."

"Who's this?" asked Jules, as she stuck out her hand, grinning at Cole.

My spirits lifted a smidge. If anyone could fix this, Jules could.

"I'm Cole," he said, shaking Jules' hand. "Did you come with them?" He scratched his temple as he looked from Jules to me and back again.

"I, uh – there's a meeting," I repeated, wishing the stained carpet we stood on would swallow me whole.

"Yes, you said that," Cole said, in an uncertain tone.

"You're more than welcome to join us," Jules said. "Do you go to St. Augustus?" Her nosiness was welcome in this moment. My tongue had tied itself in knots.

"Uh, sure. But no, I live in town." He swung back to me, his eyes veiled with confusion. A date was supposed to be two people. "Courtney?"

"This meeting just came up," I said, which It had. "We're planning a winter carnival. And you could meet some of the kids I go to school with." I hesitated to call them friends. With the exception of Margaret, anyway. My words were straight out of a Betty and Veronica comic.

"We need one more chair!" Jules yelled across the restaurant without giving Cole a chance to say no.

The two of us trudged behind her as she led the way to the table they'd secured. It was still early and there were only a few other diners in the place. She booted a few of the football team off the end of the table so Cole and I could sit together beside Ethan and Ava. I squirmed into the chair beside Cole, while Jules plopped herself down across from us, next to Jake. I put my hands flat on the table, taking a few deep breaths.

"Is this your boyfriend, Courtney?" Jake asked, shrugging off his St. Augustus jacket onto the back of his seat.

Ava's head snapped up from a few seats away. Her gaze bore a hole in my forehead.

"I-uh," I stammered. This was a bad idea. Cole would know for sure that I'd forgotten. He'd leave before I had the chance to explain. My mouth opened and closed. I couldn't think of anything smooth to say.

"This is our first date," Cole answered for me.

"Date?" Jules said. "Why didn't you say so? You guys should get your own table."

I should have insisted on our own table from the start. My

words weren't working properly. We were probably better off in a group.

"We were supposed to have a date today too, as it happens," Ethan said, giving Ava a sideways look.

"Right," Ava said, wincing. "Sorry, will you take a rain check?"

Ethan shrugged, grinning.

"We can go," I said to Cole.

"It's okay," Cole said to me, his hands folded in his lap. "I'm happy to meet your friends. You're planning a carnival?"

"We're saving the West Woods," said Ava as she leaned over Ethan to talk to Cole. "Evergreen is trying to build a road through the woods. The carnival is to raise awareness."

"Awareness?" Cole's eyebrows shot up.

"Did you know about the highway they're building?" Jules asked him.

"I'd heard," Cole said, taking a sip from his water glass that had just been topped up by the waiter. "Why do you want to stop it?"

My heart skipped a beat. Cole didn't sound as fussed about the road as the others. Perhaps between the two of us, we could convince them to let it be built.

Marcus ordered pizzas for the table. Jules clinked her fork against her water glass to silence everyone.

"We have a lot to get ready for the carnival," Jules said, loud enough for the whole table to hear. "I propose a cozy winter theme so attendees know what to wear. And we need to choose judges to select the king and queen of the carnival."

"The most important part is Courtney's," said Ava, drumming her fingers on the table. "Courtney, what's the plan for the speeches?"

My cheeks flamed. My plan was to cancel my dad as the key note speaker, although I wasn't about to say that. "It's under control," I said.

"Tell us your plan," Ava pressed, leaning into the table.

"I just need to confirm Dad can make it," I said, as I wiped my sweating palms on the red cloth napkin in my lap.

"And?" Ava asked, pressing harder. "We need more than one

speaker."

"Ava, give her a break," Jules said. "She's here with her beau, I'm sure she's got everything handled."

But Ava was right. Since I was going to cancel my dad, I had to make this look like a plausible effort. "I was thinking of asking the mayor of Evergreen to speak," I said. I had no idea who the mayor was, although I assumed he was involved in the road's approval. "And of course, Headmistress Valentine." Two pro-road people. That would be a good speaking line up.

Cole choked on his water, spitting it back into his cup.

"Are you okay?" I patted his back as he held his napkin to his mouth, catching his breath.

"Yeah," he said, clearing his throat. "Fine."

"Sounds great!" Jules said. "Get it done."

"I will," I said, as I pushed my chair back and stood. "But I owe Cole a date so we're going to go." I'd given my report and the rest didn't matter much. I was going to have two speakers who supported the road and none who didn't. That should tie things up nicely.

Cole scrambled to his feet and pulled on his coat, saluting the table. I didn't want him wrapped up in this, in my deception. I'd made the mistake of not putting him first before and I'd lost him. I wasn't going to make that mistake again.

"Have fun you two," said Jules, waving to us and smiling wide.

Ava's eyes were dark.

"Do you want to go somewhere else?" Cole asked, as we moved away from the crowded table.

I nodded. "Yes." Luigi's held too many memories. He held the door open for me as we stepped out into the late afternoon.

"Is the carnival going to be on campus?" Cole asked.

"No, it'll be at Evergreen Park. There's a skating pond."

We walked side by side along the sidewalk, past shops I'd been in many times. I was aware of the safe gap between us. I rambled. Cole lived in Evergreen. He'd know about the park.

"I haven't been there," I said. "We're in the early planning stages."

"I'll take you there now," he said. "So, you can check it out."

"Sure," I agreed, distractedly. "What do you think of the road being built?"

His reaction had been odd. I wanted to explore it.

"Husk will miss the woods." He laughed then led the way around a corner and onto a tree-lined side road, where boxy houses and square yards lined both sides. "But it doesn't affect me much one way or another. The town needs the new road. It'll be safer, keeping big trucks off the town's streets. It has to go somewhere although I get why you don't want it next to the school."

An uneasy silence hung between us. Wind whistled in the bare branches of the trees looming overhead.

"This is it," Cole said.

We'd stopped on a concrete path that led into a wide field, bordered by trees. He pointed at a large, flat area deep in the park.

"Is that the pond?" I asked.

It looked more like a tarmac of asphalt that had been shoveled. I'd imagined more of a hockey rink with boards. This skating pond was a flat oval, with sloping snow banks dipping in from all sides. Two red nets looked out of place at either end.

"People play hockey on here?" I asked.

There were no bleachers to watch from and no time clock in the park.

"Yes, come on." Any sign of his shyness melted when Cole stepped into the park. He took my hand and we jogged across the snow toward the pond, my kilt bobbing up and down with the movement.

With each step we took, the road and the carnival's importance diminished. The January sun hovered just above the horizon, casting dusky light across the snow. My new school loafers skidded down the bank. Cole tapped his foot hard against the surface of the ice, sending a wave of sound across the park.

"It's been cold for weeks," he said. "The ice is solid."

With his guidance, I stepped gingerly out onto the surface. "I'm not much of a skater," I admitted.

I'd been to arenas with my school, where we'd skated in

circles, all in the same direction. There was something wild and beautiful about this frozen pond. I'd never skated outdoors.

"I wanted to show you." Cole led me to the center of the ice, where a thick red line was drawn in marker, stretching from one bank to the other. "What do you think?"

I scrunched up my nose. "What's the line for?"

"This is where hockey games start, in the middle of the ice. I just thought it might be a good place to start our relationship."

I blinked at him. Had he just said that? It was cheesy, yet so very Cole. On this first date that was my second chance at winning him over. I smiled.

"It's a great place," I said. My knees knocked together from the cold. I'd worn jeans all winter at my last high school, not a skirt. Standing on the ice was like being inside a walk-in freezer, with any warmth in my feet being sucked through my shoes by the frozen water below.

"You're freezing, aren't you?" Cole took off his coat, wrapping it around me. It was much better against the wind than my own thin jacket. He gestured to the deepest part of the park. "You see that fence?"

"The brown one?" I squinted in the dimming light at a tall wooden fence with a gate.

"That's where I live," he said. "So, your carnival will be in my backyard."

"Will your family mind?" My heart leaped into my throat. Maybe the surrounding homeowners would complain and the event would be squashed before it even started.

"Nah, it'll be fun," he said, dashing my hopes. "Your dad's going to speak at it? Against the road?" His eyes darted between me and the fence, as though he expected Husk to burst from the gate at any moment. He took my hands, rubbing them between his.

"He might speak at the carnival," I said. "He hasn't confirmed yet. He has a busy schedule."

Cole dropped my hands and I patted the jacket he'd lent me, looking for pockets to keep the cold away.

"And you're going to invite the mayor to speak at the

carnival?" he asked, edging away from me slightly.

"Uh, yes," I replied. Had I misread our closeness? The space between us was back, as if it had been there all along.

"Would you like me to introduce you?" he asked.

"You know him?" I said.

Cole laughed, stuffing his hands into his jean pockets. "Yeah. I spend a lot of time at the city's planning office, volunteering."

Right. He'd always been interested in architecture. And here I'd been bragging at Luigi's about contacting the mayor, which I hadn't done yet. Lights on tall posts over our heads snapped on one by one around the pond as the day faded, littering circles of bluish light across the ice.

The mayor had made the deal with Valentine to buy the land. Cole was offering me the chance to get the inside scoop.

"I'm sorry I didn't mention my involvement with the planning office before," he said. "I didn't know you and your friends were protesting the road. It puts me in a strange spot, because I've been conflicted about the road."

"I'm open to hearing arguments for the road," I said, beaming.

I heard what I wanted to hear. His connection might be the key I'd been looking for.

CHAPTER EIGHT

Ava

"**Courtney was stressed** when I asked her about the speakers at the carnival," I said to Ethan as we walked back from the meeting at Luigi's.

I'd had three slices of pizza while Jules pitched her concept for decorations to the table. Courtney's reaction wasn't sitting well with me. I'd expected her to be disinterested. It wasn't that. Her answer had been shaky, as though she were conflicted.

Half of the street lamps lining the street in front of St. Augustus flickered in their cages. The other half hadn't come on and we walked past without entering the campus. I'd called ahead to tell Gran we were dropping by.

"It's like she hasn't invited any of the speakers she mentioned yet," I said.

"Senator Wallis already called Krick to talk about the road," Ethan said as he shuffled beside me, eyes on the ground. "If he comes, it'll make some noise but I don't know if it will be enough."

We didn't speak as we passed the trees of the West Woods. I let out a breath as Gran's house came into view, with its gables and gingerbread trim.

Testimony from a resident who'd lived here for many years should be more powerful than any senator from Boston. Gran's voice would be powerful at the carnival.

"If she doesn't like to leave her house much, do you think

she'll be up for this?" Ethan creased his dark eyebrows, folding his arms over his chest. I reached for the doorbell and pressed. The buzz could be heard through the door.

"That's exactly why we need her help. She doesn't like to leave her house. So, what would she do if it gets bulldozed?" Footsteps came to the door. "And I almost forgot my mom's wish."

"She wished for your gran's health, right?" he asked.

"Yes," I replied. "That's why she needs to help us. We'll take her to the carnival. Her thoughts will have an impact."

"I thought she didn't know about the fountain?" Ethan said.

"She doesn't," I replied. "So, we'll have to be convincing."

The front door swung wide. A young blond woman stood on the threshold, with an oval face and puffy cheeks. She wore a smart taupe dress and shiny brown shoes.

I blinked at her. Gran had a revolving door of housekeepers but I'd never met this one.

"I'm Ava," I said, in a hurried tone. "This is Ethan. We're here to see my gran."

"She talks about you all the time," the woman said. "She's in the parlor. Come in."

I took Ethan's hand and we stepped inside together, down the hall to Gran's sitting room where she sat in her usual corner under a colorful tiffany lamp hanging from the ceiling. She had a thick novel on her lap, propped up on the blanket tucked around her legs and into the sides of her wheelchair. Her smile was as bright as ever and her lips were the same pale pink as the lace-trimmed dress she wore. Gran always dressed in freshly pressed clothing, even when she didn't go out.

"Happy New Year, Ava," Gran greeted me, putting her book down. "And welcome to you too, Ethan."

"Sorry I didn't come by sooner," I said, bending over to give her a hug.

"Oh, I know young people are too busy to visit an old lady like me." There was a twinkle in her eye.

"You don't look a day over forty," Ethan crooned.

Gran laughed. "Are you here to ask for money?"

"That depends, are you looking to adopt two students with

expensive tastes?" Ethan pointed to himself and me, with a wide grin on his face.

"Ethan, be serious." I gave an exasperated sigh. Asking him to be serious was like asking him to completely overhaul his personality. We were there on important business, I had to at least make the suggestion.

"We came to talk to you about the woods," I said, settling myself on Gran's flower-stitched couch, patting the stiff square cushion beside me for Ethan to join. "You must know about the plans for the highway?"

"Yes, I was consulted." Gran folded her hands in her lap.

"We've joined forces with some students and a teacher. We're going to stop it, Gran." My voice warbled. "We want you to speak at the carnival we're putting on, against the road."

Gran's lower lip protruded, just a bit. She had something to say. "I was planning to talk to you about this, although you've beat me to it. I've known about the road for a few months," she said.

My stomach lurched. They weren't going to listen to her. She'd already tried.

"I'm not fighting it," she said. "The state will purchase my home and land for a fair price. I'll move into the seniors' care facility in town and play cards." She laughed.

Her words rattled around in my head.

"Wait, you're okay with the road, and the woods getting plowed?" Ethan asked.

"Everything changes." Gran smiled. "And the real estate market is depressed in this town. I'd rather leave my daughter and granddaughter money than a house they can't sell."

"Aunt Mia and I don't need your money," I said, as I grappled with what she'd told us.

"This house is beautiful," Ethan said.

"I love this house," Gran said. "I've spent the best years of my life in it, however there's no option to sell. Nobody wants to live this far from town and next to a busy road. The town will build this road whether or not I sell them my home. I'm sorry for the inconvenience you'll have at the school, but I'm told it helps St. Augustus financially. In a year and a half, you'll both be heading off to college. The school's campus will still hold your wonderful memories, even with the construction."

I wiped a tear of frustration from my cheek. She'd made up her mind.

"I'm not moving far," she said, gently. "Will you visit me in town?"

"You don't have to give up your house," I said. There had to be another way.

"I *want* to give up my house," Gran corrected me. "I have a constant parade of strangers as housekeepers. I suppose I'm not very good company these days. None of them stay for long."

"Gran," I said. "These woods, they're special."

She must know something was different about them.

Her laugh caught me off guard, zinging through me.

"What is it with your generation and wanting to save trees?" She smiled. "Trees are cut down to make progress. Once, there were trees over the whole town, instead of the town."

"What about the fountain?" My heart pumped in my chest. I couldn't stop the words from coming out. Ethan darted a look at me sideways. We hadn't rehearsed this part.

"Your mother used to talk about such nonsense too." Gran clucked her tongue. "Yet I've never seen it, and Mariam, rest her soul, won't miss it."

I let out a long breath.

"I take it you've found Mariam's fountain?" Gran's voice dipped as she raised an eyebrow at me. "I should like to see it before I die."

"It-it's only visible to students," I said.

Gran's tinny laughter broke the silence. "Such nonsense!" she said. "You almost had me there, Ava. Did you get that from Mariam's diaries? She was always such a dreamer."

My shoulders slumped. If mom told her about the fountain, and couldn't convince her it was real, we weren't going to be successful either. We didn't have proof.

"You don't need to worry about me, Ava." Gran smiled. "Besides, I'm protecting your inheritance."

I rushed to her side. I didn't care about her money. And of

course, I wanted her to be comfortable. Happy. If the seniors' home could do that for her, I could get behind it. There was nothing more we could do. We had to find support somewhere else.

CHAPTER NINE

Ava

Ethan and I trudged back to campus with few words between us after visiting Gran. I was so deep in thought I didn't even look at the West Woods as we passed it. As we reached the last streetlamp before the campus, a shadow fell over my eyes and grew until we were both engulfed by it.

"Do you have Ms. Krick's blue rock with you?" I whispered, as a majestic set of wings blocked out the moonlight, circling high above us.

"Yes." Ethan reached into his pocket, producing the stone, which sported a sea-blue halo of light in the palm of his hand. "There it goes, glowing again."

While he stared at it, a flapping sound from just over our heads grabbed my attention.

"Ethan!" I tugged at his arm, but my warning was too late. Izzy dropped low with his claws bared. His sharp talons were pointed right at Ethan's face.

"What the heck!" Ethan scrambled backward, swatting at Izzy as the owl set down on his head, his wings spread like a tightrope walker keeping his balance with a pole.

"Get off, you crazy bird," Ethan yelled.

Krick's stone fell from his grip and clattered to the ground as I leaped into the fray, trying to pull Izzy off Ethan from behind. I pressed my arms in on either side of the owl, grabbing only a puffy layer of feathers, which came off in my hands in clumps.

"Stop! You're making him panic!" Ethan yelled. "He's digging in his claws!" Ethan's fingers scratched at Izzy's legs and he managed to get the bird off his head as I took a step back. Izzy scrabbled onto Ethan's shoulders, swaying off kilter. The owl screeched and flapped his wings as his razor-sharp claws shredded through Ethan's thin jacket and tore a hole in his cardigan, which started to unravel like a ball of yarn.

"Shoo!" I swung my arms at the out-of-control bird, making contact with the side of his beak. My hand smarted from the impact. Izzy made a guttural noise in his throat, then his golden eyes opened wide, his neck corkscrewing in my direction. He looked just as surprised at their entanglement as Ethan was. He spread his wings, pushing off Ethan's shoulders to launch himself into the air, and then he was gone.

Ethan doubled over, gasping for air.

I rushed to him, my mouth agape at the thin trickles of dark red snaking like rivers down Ethan's forehead.

"Can owls carry rabies?" was what popped out of my mouth. "You need to see Bessie."

The girls' dorm mother, Bessie, was also the school's nurse.

Ethan wiped his eyes with the back of his hand, staring at the crimson smears on his knuckles. "He attacked me," he said.

"I don't think he meant to hurt you. He lost his balance." I poked around Ethan's shoulders, taking stock of the damage. Izzy's claws had slashed Ethan's jacket, sweater, and shirt, but the scratches on his skin were shallow.

Ethan searched his scalp with his fingers. "Is it bad?"

I squinted at his forehead. "Mostly superficial. Still, you need to get checked out. He's a wild animal, who knows what's on his claws." I cringed.

"You're not making me feel better," he muttered. He bent low to retrieve Krick's pendant from the pavement. It had lost its luminescence and sat dull in his palm.

"You still want that thing?" I scrunched my nose at the rock. "If it calls Izzy, maybe we should just get rid of it?"

"Maybe it'll come in handy," he said, slipping it into the pocket of his tattered jacket. "We can summon him to attack the guys operating the bulldozers when they come to break ground."

"I'm good as new," Ethan assured me, as he slipped into his desk at the beginning of calculus class mid-morning the next day. "Apparently only mammals can carry rabies and owls aren't mammals, so I didn't even need a shot."

Other than a hairline scratch across his forehead, which was forming a ruby-colored scab, he looked none the worse. He wore a fresh, clean uniform with no rips.

"You couldn't text me?" I swatted him with my notebook. "I was worried when you weren't in class."

He'd been a bit disoriented by the time we found Bessie the night before and she'd waved me off, sending me to my room so I didn't miss curfew.

"Bessie said I could sleep in if I needed to," he said, shrugging. "I took her up on it."

"You were that tired?" Ethan got up before seven even on weekends.

"I can always sleep in if it means missing class," Ethan said, smirking.

"Did you tell Bessie about Izzy?" I dropped my voice as I sat at my desk.

"I told her it was an owl. You said yourself he's a wild animal," he said, wincing as he slid his books out of his backpack. "I didn't feel the need to call him by name. That felt unfair somehow. The school called animal control."

"What?" Class was about to start.

"There must be lots of owls in the woods," he said. "And he's smart. They won't catch him."

"Open your texts to page one-fifteen," Mr. Chase said, as he strolled into the room.

I fished my book out of my backpack, but promptly forgot what page Mr. Chase wanted us to read. A knot formed in the pit of my stomach. Would Izzy know he was being hunted? And what would animal control do to him if they caught him? Dogs who attacked people were usually put down, no questions asked. What did they do to owls? I shivered, peering over at Ethan's book to copy his page number.

"You stole the stone and sentenced Izzy to death!" Ms. Krick burst into the classroom, wearing a plum colored skirt and blazer. Her eyes rested on Ethan. "We have to save him." Her arms stretched wide, as if she were an owl herself.

Mr. Chase stood in Ms. Krick's path. "It seems a lot of things need saving, these days, Matilda," he said, addressing her like he would to sooth a child having a tantrum.

She pointed at Ethan, her hand shaking like a leaf. "It's him! The Roth boy! He did it."

Mr. Chase took her by her shoulders and spun her around to face him. "Matilda, what are you talking about?" He looked at her over his round spectacles. His sandy brown hair fell into his eyes.

He pushed her toward the door, where their heated voices could be heard from the hall. "You can't just burst in like that," he said. "You're already on thin ice with Moira. You've got to get a grip. The students will definitely report your behavior."

Better than that. Several students had their smart phones pointed at the doorway, recording.

"He's controlling Izzy!" Ms. Krick shrieked.

The class gathered around Ethan's desk. Ethan flinched as Ms. Krick's sobs echoed in the hall.

"Ethan got attacked by an owl last night. You know, the one Ms. Krick talks to," Marcus said loudly.

"Ethan was attacked?" asked Jules, her hands on her hips as she spun to face me. "Why am I only hearing about this now?"

"Maybe when they catch the owl, we can tame him and make him our football team mascot," Marcus suggested.

"Owls are icky," Jules said, shaking her head.

"Our team mascot is already an owl," Margaret said. "Even if it's a silver one."

"Sure, but a real one we can train to do tricks and stuff," added Jake, as he got in on the conversation.

"Just go read the pages Mr. Chase told us to," I said, waving them off.

Ethan's face was ashen.

"Ms. Krick was right. I should have kept Izzy out of my

report," he said to me when the others had dispersed. "I have to warn him. I can't let him get caught."

"He won't," I said, echoing what Ethan had said earlier but my voice shook.

"Class, take your seats." Mr. Chase came over to Ethan's desk and squatted beside him. "Ethan, do you know what Ms. Krick was talking about?" His brow was creased into a deep valley.

"No," Ethan said, his eyes trained on his desk.

Mr. Chase would find out soon enough that Ethan was lying. That the scratches on his face had been made by an owl. Bessie wasn't known for her discretion.

"I'm not feeling well," said Ethan. "May I be excused?"

"Yes," Mr. Chase replied. "And if you know anything about Ms. Krick's owl, or if you can fix this, then please do that."

"I'll try," Ethan said. He slipped out of his desk, hugging his backpack to his chest. He gave me an almost imperceptible jerk of his head, aimed at the door. He wanted me to follow.

"Uh, Mr. Chase?" I said, as I raised my hand. "Ethan did get attacked by an owl last night. He was in rough shape and hasn't fully recovered. I can take him to Bessie."

"I think Mr. Roth can handle himself." Mr. Chase looked down his nose at me.

I slumped into my seat, stuck. I should have waited a minute, then asked to go to the restroom. It was too late, now. Where was Ethan headed?

When the lunch bell rang, I hurried to the main building, rushing up the curved steps to the student lounge then scanned the tables at the cafeteria. Ethan wasn't in any of our usual haunts.

I dialed his number and listened to it ring as I entered the winding stone hall that led to the library. "Come on, pick up," I said into my phone. It went to voicemail after three rings, so I hung up.

"Where are you??" I texted. I frowned at my phone screen, waiting for it to tell me he'd read my message. It didn't. My head pounded as I peered around the shelves of books in the library, staying out of the line of sight of the librarian's desk, but he wasn't there.

Instead, I'd come face to face with Courtney.

"I saw him go into the woods," she said, breathlessly.

My back bristled. Of course, I'd thought of that. He was talking about warning Izzy but I didn't think he'd go in broad daylight. If Courtney saw him, who else had?

"I can show you where," she offered. Her curls fell across one eye. Her voice was quiet. I made a beeline for the foyer, with Courtney in tow. I pushed down my reservations. I'd find Ethan faster with her help.

I brushed my way past small groups of kids in the foyer and almost ran straight into Jules.

"I saw Ethan going into the woods," Jules said. "I tried to find you to tell you."

"I know," I said in a low voice, looking back at Courtney. "Can you put this in our room for me?" I thrust my backpack into her arms. Jules had seen him too. Was I the only one on campus who had missed this while I was running around looking for Ethan in all the places he *should* have been?

"He'll come back, just wait for him." Jules slung my pack over her available shoulder. "You're not doing him any favors by chasing after him. You'll draw more attention. What's gotten into him anyway?"

"If we go behind the sports complex and double back to the West Building, only people looking out the windows would see us," Courtney said. "And it's lunchtime. The West Building should be empty."

"He went to look for Izzy," I said to Jules, as if that would explain everything. "And I'm not leaving him out there. Izzy sort of attacked him last night. Sorry I didn't tell you, it was late. We think it was an accident, but I still don't think Ethan should be alone, in case something else happens. Cover for me if I'm not back?"

She wouldn't need to cover for Courtney. I was going to send Courtney away as soon as she showed me where Ethan went.

I didn't wait for Jules to react, I just left. Courtney followed behind me like a stray dog I couldn't shake. I had no idea where Izzy would be or if he was in the woods at all.

"Can Ethan talk to Izzy or something?" she called, as I ducked behind the east wall of the sports complex. "Does Izzy understand?"

I put a finger to my lips. She was going to get us both busted. My heart raced as we hit the border of the woods. Winter branches grabbed at my kilt, scratching my exposed knees above my socks. There was no path. My shoes sank into the snow, which hadn't melted in the shade. It was only ankle deep, but it was enough to freeze my toes. We'd picked our way far enough that we were behind the West Building. If anyone looked out of the second-floor windows, they'd see us.

"Are you headed for the clearing?" Courtney asked.

I walked fast, but she caught up, like a nymph. What did she know about the clearing?

"I don't think that's where he went. He should be somewhere right over there." She pointed deeper into the woods.

"Shh..." I held out my arm to block her way. I gasped as a shower of dead twigs and leaves assaulted us from above. Courtney shrieked, swatting at her own hair as dried leaves decorated her head like a crown.

I resisted the urge to scream with her. There didn't seem to be any immediate threat. Dirt rained down on my face. I used my sleeve to wipe it off. I looked up to see where a scrabbling sound came from. There was movement, something larger than a bird. I squinted up through the branches.

"Is that Ethan?" Courtney asked, placing her palms against the lichen-covered trunk of the large tree that towered over us.

I craned my neck to see past the web of branches, stretching up to the sky.

"Ethan!" I called, as his white running shoe found a higher branch then hoisted his body up. "Be careful!" I winced as he edged himself out onto a thick branch, which had a large clump of twigs and matted leaves at the end.

"Izzy led me to his nest," he called. "I'm almost there."

I held my breath. The branch he crawled on was higher than the main building. He hugged one arm around the tree's thick branch, stretching out with the other. If he fell, there wouldn't be much left of him when he hit the ground. He found a twig to hold onto and swung his legs down on either side of the branch so he was seated. Leaning forward, he stretched to peer into the mess.

"What's in the nest?" Courtney called to him.

I dragged my gaze away from him as Courtney kicked at the damp leaves and snow under the tree, making a pile. I rubbed my neck. It had cricked from my head being upturned.

"What are you doing?" I stared at her, with my hands on my hips. I should have sent her away already, not that she would have gone. My knees trembled. I didn't like Ethan being up so high. I imagined him hitting the ground with a splash of limbs.

"I'm making a softer landing, just in case," Courtney said, working quickly.

So, I wasn't the only one who thought this was going to end badly. That didn't comfort me. Helping Courtney would be better than standing there waiting, playing the worst case scenario over and over in my head. I bent as low as I could, conscious of my kilt riding up in the back. I gathered debris that had fallen, pushing the scattered branches together to add to Courtney's makeshift safety net.

"He won't fall," I said, more to myself than to Courtney, perhaps to convince us both.

The two of us worked together, adding to the pile. The branches overhead still rustled, but I couldn't look. We'd been gone a long time. Our afternoon classes would have started by now. We'd cleared the area around us of loose branches.

"Give me a hand with this? We can add it to the pile," Courtney said. She had her arms around a low shrub and her face was red with effort. I scrambled over, grabbing hold of the base of its branches. "Pull."

And I did. Grunting, my body leaned away from the shrub at a forty-five-degree angle.

"I think it's moving," I said. Had I imagined the few inches of give?

"What are you two doing?"

I jumped at the sound of Ethan's voice as he hopped to the ground, his feet landing squarely. We'd been so absorbed in making a soft landing that I hadn't seen him climb down.

Courtney and I were still pulling, but the roots of the shrub gave way and we were thrown back, landing in a heap at Ethan's feet. The dense shrub followed our arc, smacking its wet whips in my face.

"Er..." Ethan towered over us. He had paper scraps sticking out of his pockets and from the top of his cardigan. "Killer shrub?" he asked, pulling the attacking bush off me and tossing it aside.

"We were saving you," I mumbled, rolling over on the snow-covered ground and pushing myself to a sitting position.

"Oh?" He folded his arms across his chest.

Courtney got to her feet and offered me a hand, which I ignored. Instead, I heaved myself up under my own steam.

"What's all that paper?" Courtney asked, pointed at his stuffed sweater.

"I put them there so my hands would be free to climb down," he said, pulling out the slips of paper from his pockets and his sleeve, consolidating them in his hands.

"What do they say?" asked Courtney, at his shoulder.

"Ethan," I said. A warning. "Maybe we could read them later?"

Courtney crossed her arms. "What? I have just as much right to be here as you."

Her words crawled up my neck like spiders. Even under the shade of the trees around us, her green eyes flashed with a challenge I'd seen before. The Courtney I'd known was in there, buried under all her helpfulness.

"You remember," I said in a whisper. An accusation.

"Yes, but I'm sorry. I'm sorry for all of it. I made a wish. That's why -" She stopped, looking from me to Ethan and back again.

I forced myself to hold her gaze. My mind whirred with activity.

A stiff breeze came up, lifting the papers Ethan held and scattering them across the ground around the tree. We mobilized, scrambling to gather them.

"Don't let them get wet, it'll smudge the ink." Courtney had a stack of the weathered pages in her arms, enough to fill a book.

She kneeled in the snow, gathering more. "These are from Isaac Young's journals, right?"

My eyes locked with Ethan's. "She remembers," I whispered. I couldn't fathom what that meant.

CHAPTER TEN

Ava

"Ethan should take the pages," I said to Courtney. "He's excused from class, we aren't."

She had most of the pages Ethan had recovered from his climb clutched in her hands. I'd only managed to grab a few. I glanced down at the few pages I held and sucked in a breath. The top one was an ink sketch of the fountain. We'd hit the motherload.

"So, we'll tell Bessie we're sick," she said. "Aren't you dying to find out why Izzy wanted us to have them?"

I looked over at Ethan for help, but he only shrugged. He missed class all the time. But I didn't. We were interrupted by a loud static sound, followed by an unintelligible voice on a walkie-talkie, coming from the edge of the woods, which was our way out. The blood drained from my face.

"Animal control," I whispered. "They're here."

"Where's Izzy?" Courtney asked.

"He flew in short bursts from tree to tree to lead me here," Ethan said. "As soon as I started climbing up, he took off." He pointed to the sky.

"I hope he's smart enough not to come back," Courtney said.

"And we need to be smart enough to get out of here," I added, shivering.

I had no jacket. I shooed Ethan and Courtney deeper into the trees. We were breaking a school rule just by being in the woods, not to mention skipping class.

"This isn't the way out," Ethan said, jogging along behind me as I barreled through the trees, which were close together.

"Do you want to get caught?" I asked.

The back of my neck prickled. A twig snapped off to our right and I spun around. A white clad figure moved through the trees a short distance away. How many people had they sent to look for Izzy?

"Animal Control isn't going to bother us," Ethan said. "Last time I looked, we weren't animals. Why would they care if we're in the woods?"

I rounded on him. "We're not supposed to be in the woods. It's a school rule, which you both know." I looked pointedly at Courtney.

"I don't think Animal Control cares about arbitrary school rules," Courtney said. She'd dropped a bit behind, watching the figure in the woods.

"Ms. Krick is probably out here, too, looking for Izzy." I crossed my arms. There wasn't time to be arguing about this.

"She probably is," Ethan said. "And she'd be pleased we were trying to help Izzy, although I'd rather not see her. She might try to confiscate these pages."

I couldn't tell if he agreed or if he was appeasing me, but at least we were moving again.

I lied to Bessie when we got back. She was waiting at my room when I went to change my mud-stained knee socks for a fresh pair. I'd been reported as skipping class and she'd come to find me. My cheeks flamed as I told her I hadn't been feeling well, but that I'd recovered.

I don't know what excuse Courtney gave or even if she was questioned. I didn't let on that we'd been together.

Courtney was already in her seat when I got to History, our last class of the afternoon. When the final bell rang, I hightailed it to my room to shed my uniform and put on leggings and a hoodie. I hadn't warmed up since we'd been in the woods. I tugged on the railing to speed myself along as I took the stairs to the student lounge.

Ethan was in our usual spot on the far side by the windows. Izzy's pages were spread all over our low table, while Courtney hovered over his shoulder.

"How did she know we were meeting here?" I muttered as I approached.

Ethan threw his head back and laughed at something she said. I was still out of hearing range. I clenched and released my fists. There were only a handful of students in the huge space, but Ethan should have been more careful with Izzy's pages. They were unprotected on the table.

Courtney saw me first, waving me over like she had the right to invite me to their cozy gathering. "Ava, come see this."

Ethan leaped to his feet, wearing my favorite lopsided smile.

My pout remained.

"Courtney made a wish, just like you did," he said, defending her. "She wished for the strength to do everything necessary to be team captain. She wanted to pad her college resume but then she was bound to that wish by the fountain. It made her treat you the way she did. She couldn't stop herself. She didn't mean any of it. She wants to help us."

I gaped at him. He'd forgiven her so easily. Could I do the same? Courtney's wish had turned her into the girl I'd met. I'd undone all that when I'd wished her away. Did she know about my wish? She was different now, unaffected by the fountain's reach.

"It's true," Courtney said, swinging around Ethan's chair and sitting beside him. "I've been walking around with this secret cooped up inside. I thought I'd gone nuts for a bit but you guys know all about the fountain. So now we can figure out what to do, together." Her smile was so wide it hurt me to look at it.

"Great," I managed to say, directing daggers at Ethan.

"Relax, Ava," he said, reaching for my hand and pulling me to sit on his other side. "She's cool."

I clenched my teeth. Courtney most certainly was not cool.

"Ethan told me about your wish," she said, as I braced for the impact. "And I really don't know how to thank you. I wished for a chance to undo all the horrible stuff I did and then that wish came true. And you did that, whether you knew what you were doing, or not. You made my wish for me. How did you know?"

I checked over my shoulder, confirming that the other students in the lounge weren't paying attention to our conversation.

"I didn't," I said.

Her thanks didn't make sense. I'd made the wish for my own selfish reasons. Courtney went out of her way to make me feel unwelcome at St. Augustus when I'd arrived. Just thinking about the night I'd found the fountain sent hot prickles up my back. I'd made my wish out of spite and I'd wanted to take it back ever since. Yet somehow, I'd given Courtney what she wanted. How could that be?

"There's a bunch of pages here on the fountain and how it works," said Ethan.

He wasn't bothered by my inner turmoil. He waved his hand over the left side of the scraps of parchment, as if my whole world hadn't just been turned upside down. Each page was laid in a grid on the table like a card game of concentration.

"We've already figured a lot of this out," Ethan said. "The fountain only appears to students and you can't see it after you make a wish. But look at this." He plucked up a piece of paper that didn't match the others. It was yellowed with age, its corners crisp. A weathered envelope made from the same paper lay beside it. The handwriting on the address and the page was loopy, more feminine than Isaac's angles.

"Isaac Young had a child, a daughter," Courtney blurted out. "The letter is from the mother, dated 1920. The envelope was still sealed before we opened it."

I'd missed a lot.

"He created the fountain," Ethan said. "Maybe his descendants would have some kind of control over it."

Courtney shrugged. It was the least enthusiastic she'd been since I'd arrived.

"You don't agree?" I was more than happy to point out her dissent and more than annoyed Ethan had shared all this with her without waiting for me.

"It couldn't hurt to find out. His daughter would be really old by now, probably dead," she said.

"If Isaac Young never opened the letter, maybe he didn't even know." I picked up the envelope and turned it over to read the return address. "M. Hastings. This address is in Evergreen. We can go see the house. Maybe whoever lives there now will know something."

Courtney smiled at something on her phone. "Let me know what you find," she said. "I've got to go."

CHAPTER ELEVEN

Courtney

I didn't care if I was being eager. Cole texted me when I was in the student lounge with Ava and Ethan, asking when we could get together. I invited myself over to his house and nearly skipped all the way there.

I'd almost forgotten myself, helping Ethan. I also almost forgot that I wanted the fountain gone as I turned toward the park.

I was thankful for Ava's wish, but the nightmares of the other timelines the wall had shown me haunted my sleep. It was best if it all just went away, so I could concentrate on Cole.

It was nearing dusk when I got to Evergreen Park and spotted the house Cole had shown me. I let myself in through the iron gate in the wooden fence, wincing as its hinges creaked. I picked my way over snow drifts in the side yard to get to the front. Maybe once I was on more familiar terms with his family, I'd come and go through this back yard. It was much closer to the school than walking around the block.

The porch steps to Cole's house were flanked by two wooden pillars, painted olive green to match his house. There were wrought iron sconces on the top of each post but the lamps weren't on. I ran my fingers over a brass plaque affixed to one of the wooden columns. It declared the house to be a protected historical landmark.

I smiled, remembering Cole's love of architecture. My limbs pulsed with nervous energy. I wanted to learn everything about him. Taking a deep breath, I pressed the black button beside the door, triggering a jarring buzzing sound, one that only old doorbells made. Husk's barks echoing on the other side of the door eased me. My trusted ally.

Quick footsteps clicked behind the door. My stomach clenched. Those weren't Cole's footsteps. I painted on my best meet-the-parents smile, running my tongue over my teeth. The door opened an inch and a woman's face appeared in the crack. Her blond waves curled under at her chin. Husk's muzzle poked in the open space at my knees, licking my hand where I extended it to him.

"Yes?" the woman asked, relaxing her grip on the door and opening it wider.

"She's here for me, Mom," Cole called, his feet thundering down a central staircase that spilled into the foyer.

His mom's forehead crinkled as she stepped back. She took Husk by the collar, pulling him away from the door. His front paws lifted off the ground as he tried to reach me with his panting tongue.

"Well, Husk seems to know you," his mother mused, looking from the dog to me.

He'd grown so much in a year. And he'd known me from our first meeting. I cocked my head to one side, considering.

Cole swept in and kissed his mom on the cheek. "Mom, this is Courtney. She goes to St. Augustus."

"Nice to meet you, Mrs. Coffman," I said, bending to ruffle the fur at the back of Husk's neck. I was glad I'd shed my short uniform kilt in favor of sensible jeans as Cole's mom raked her eyes over me. I stepped inside, onto polished dark hardwood floors. The foyer was paneled with the same rich wood tones as St. Augustus' main office.

Cole eyed me curiously and then my stomach sank. I wasn't supposed to know his last name was Coffman. I was terrible at this secret-keeping business.

"We're going for a w-a-l-k," he said.

I smiled at his attempt to hide our intent from Husk as long as possible, while thinking of ways to backpedal from my mistake.

"You're welcome to stay here and watch a movie or something, if you like," Mrs. Coffman offered, tucking her perfectly coifed hair behind one ear. "I'll make popcorn."

She let Husk go, under Cole's care, and closed the front door behind me.

"What do you think?" Cole asked me.

I blinked. I'd been focused on seeing him again and we'd talked about going for a walk. Somehow watching a movie together felt like a much more serious date. His mother took a respectful step back.

"I'll leave it up to you two," she said. Her voice had a sing-song quality. She eased herself away from our conversation, disappearing down the hall.

"It doesn't matter to me what we do," I said, shrugging. And it didn't. I hadn't stopped smiling since he'd come down the stairs, even though my stomach was in knots, and he might think I was stalking his family if I knew more than I should. "Husk looks like he wants to go out though."

Cole laughed. "Well, if the king of the household wants that, who are we to refuse? I'll get my coat."

He ducked into a small alcove off the foyer and returned wearing a red ball cap. His red curls poked out from under the hat. He grabbed Husk's leash from an iron hook on the wall and clipped it onto his collar. Husk's tail beat against the red flowered wallpaper of the entryway, wagging with anticipation.

The doorbell buzzed again, its rattling ring grating through me.

"I've got it!" Cole called to the other room then opened the heavy wooden door.

I gasped. Ava and Ethan stood on the doorstep, wearing thick woolen coats and holding hands. What were they doing here? Ava had on a knit beanie, with an oversized fur pompom on top. They looked as cute as the winter-loving couples in the L.L. Bean catalogue.

"Uh, hi?" I said gaping. I wondered if they'd followed me.

"What are you doing here?" It was Ava, asking me the question that was on my own lips, her eyes wide.

"We were just going out for a walk," Cole replied, looking at me. "Is this going to be another group date?" He raised his eyebrows.

"No," I blurted. I hadn't set this up but I could see how it looked. I wasn't trying to sabotage my time with him. "I didn't tell them I was coming. I have no idea why they're even here."

My hands were on my hips. I squared my shoulders to Ava and Ethan. I was looking forward to spending this time with Cole.

"This was the address on the letter," Ava said, holding it up, although Cole was too far away to read the writing on the paper. "M. Hastings lived at 24 Arbor Street. We came to see what we could find out about the lady who wrote this letter to the school's founder. Is this your house?"

"Yeah," said Cole. "And my dad taught me most of its history. We had the house recognized by the historical society, so the list of all its occupants was part of the requirements. I don't remember a Hastings, although we have all the records."

"Is someone else here, Cole?" his mom called from somewhere in the back of the house.

"Just a few more friends, Mom!" he answered then turned back to Ava and Ethan, who still stood on the steps as Ava's shoulders shook with the cold. "Why are you looking for someone named Hastings?"

"We're researching Isaac Young – er – as part of trying to stop the road. To save the West Woods," Ava replied. "Can we come in?" She stepped over the threshold and started unbuttoning her coat.

"Uh, sure." Cole waved Ethan to come in and dropped Husk's leash to close the door against the wind. "And we can ask my mom for the records, but maybe just tell her you're researching the town. The West Woods project is a bit of a hot button around here."

"Oh?" Ava asked, her eyes narrowed at Cole.

Mrs. Coffman's heels clicked into the foyer. "Are your friends coming in?" she asked.

"Yeah," he said, his hands in his pockets. "This is Ethan and Ava. They're from St. Augustus as well. They're doing a project on historical buildings in Evergreen and they're interested in the history of our house. Can we take a look at our Historical Place records?"

Cole's mom smiled broadly. "Of course, come on in." She waved us into an oversized dining room. Their mahogany dining table had a dozen chairs around it, its surface gleaming. I winced as Ava tossed her coat onto the back of one of the burgundy upholstered chairs, pulling another one out to sit down. "It's Cole's dad, Robert, you should really talk with, but Cole knows a lot about this house too. I'll just go get the files then I'll make you all some hot chocolate."

"Thanks, Mrs. -" said Ethan, as he cocked his head expectantly. He sat at the dining room table next to Ava, leaving his coat on.

"It's Brenda, please," Cole's mom called over her shoulder as she brushed past me on her way out of the room.

I stood in the archway to the dining room, with one foot in and one foot out in the hall. What were the chances that Isaac Young's girlfriend once lived in Cole's house? Ava and Ethan were dragging Cole into their quest. My stomach twisted. Husk padded up beside me and sat with his head sagging on his outstretched front paws. Cole had put the leash back on the hook by the door.

"Sorry, buddy," I said, kneeling to scratch behind his ear as he whined, nuzzling into my hand.

"Here are the files." Brenda re-entered the room with a small stack of manila folders and put them in front of Cole, who'd taken the seat at the end of the table next to Ava. "Mind you don't crease them. And I'll bring the hot chocolate when you're done. Dad wouldn't be happy if you spill."

"Thanks, Mom," Cole mumbled. "I think we can handle not wrecking the papers." He then opened the top folder.

This semester was going to be the longest I'd ever been away from my family, at least in this reality, and being in this house reminded me of mine. My dog, my mom, and the savory smell of the Coffman's earlier supper – hamburgers, maybe? A wave of homesickness hit me as I crouched beside Husk. Neither in nor out. My dog at home wasn't allowed in the dining room either. I wondered what my parents would think about me being off campus, at a boy's house, even if his mom was home. They'd like Cole, if they'd give him a chance.

"Courtney, are you going to join us?" Ethan asked.

He and Ava looked my way. Cole's eyes had a light to them as he flipped through pages and pages of printed paper. He loved this house and it was beautiful. Wooden beams ran lengthwise on the dining room ceiling. Its gray and silver paisley wallpaper was modern, although the house must have been at least a hundred years old. I thought back to the letter that had been in Izzy's nest. It had come from this house. Cole's house.

Husk whimpered as I stood and stepped over the threshold. He couldn't follow.

"Our house was placed on the National Register of Historic Places about ten years ago," Cole said, without looking up at me as I slipped into the chair next to him, settling in against the tall upholstered back. "Obviously, I didn't help with the original filing but I've kept up with the reports we submit that show how we're maintaining it. My dad's pretty into the history of Evergreen and I love all the old buildings here. I plan to study architecture in college. I already volunteer at City Hall in the planning office."

"What do you do there?" asked Ethan, leaning forward on his elbows.

"Not much," Cole said with a sheepish smile, his eyes shaded by the ball cap he'd put on for our walk. "Mostly filing but it'll look good on my college application."

I stared at Cole, wanting to soak in every detail he shared. I'd been blinded by the fountain the first time we'd met. I'd never even been to this house before.

"You said there was a list of families who'd lived in the house?" Ava asked, leaning in.

"Yes. It's here." Cole pulled out a sheet of paper with a flourish of his wrist.

Ava rose and moved to look over his shoulder. I jumped up from my seat and leaned over his other side.

"Any Hastings?" Ethan asked. "It would have been sometime

in the nineteen twenties, maybe earlier. The letter is dated 1920."

Cole ran his finger down the page, where names were neatly typed, with dates beside them. He got to the bottom, then shook his head. "No Hastings in any time period."

"It says a family called Jackman lived here from 1920 until 1940," Ava said, chewing on her lower lip.

"Sorry I couldn't be more help." Cole said, leaving the page on top of the file. "What was the letter about?"

My spirits brightened. The letter was a dead end. No need for Cole and his house or his parents to get involved.

"The letter claims Isaac Young had a daughter," Ava said, eyeing me as I wiped the smile off my face. "One he may not have known about."

"Are you trying to find her?" Cole asked, frowning.

"Just following a hunch." Ethan left his seat and was standing by the oversized sideboard by the wall. It was a massive piece of furniture as tall as Ethan's chest. It was made from the same dark wood as the table and chairs. Atop it were arranged two tea sets. One was made of flowered china; one was plainer and made from glass. A domed display case stood between them, featuring a rusty-red pendant, propped up on a black velvet nest. "What's this?"

"It's just a stone my dad likes," Cole said. "It's an unusual color, so he supposes it's valuable, but Mom said it's just iron deposits in the rock that makes it red."

Ethan pressed his hand against the glass case, leaning in to examine it. Was he interested in jewelry?

"Just don't leave any fingerprints," Cole said. "My dad's particular about it." He gave a nervous laugh.

"Sorry." Ethan took his hand away and rubbed the glass with the sleeve of his coat.

The pendant was oval, with smooth edges, but even its color was unremarkable. Its orange undertones clashed with the deep ruby colors in the rest of Cole's dining room.

"Where did he get it?" Ethan hadn't taken his eyes off the rock.

"I've never really asked him," Cole said, scratching his head.

"I'll ask him when he gets home tonight."

"No!" Ava said, quickly. "We've taken up enough of your time. No need to ask your dad about it, Ethan just likes... rocks." She grabbed her coat from the back of the chair she sat in and then prodded Ethan.

"Sorry I haven't been much help." Cole got to his feet.

"Thanks for letting us intrude on you guys," Ethan said.

Ava's gaze darted over the walls. They were casing the place but for what? Signs of the mysterious M. Hastings?

We walked toward voices in the hall.

"He attacked a student," a deep voice said.

I stumbled on the edge of the dining room rug. Who attacked a student? What student?

"They've been looking for him all day."

I was all ears. Cole and I going for a walk right now might be a bad idea, if a student had been attacked. Ava and Ethan probably shouldn't walk back to campus either. I grabbed Ava's sleeve.

"What happened, Dad?" Cole asked.

His father had arrived home from work and was talking with Brenda in the hall. He was everything I'd imagined about Cole's family, wearing a suit, tie, and long black overcoat. He had rubber pull-on soles over his dress shoes and sported a neatly trimmed beard.

"It's that blasted owl again," Robert Coffman said, with a heavy sigh. "He's gone berserk. I've been saying that for decades. *Decades*, mind you. What kind of owl lives that long?"

Was he talking about Izzy? It was a strange coincidence, but I was glad to hear there wasn't a real attacker out there. First the letter led to Cole's house, now this.

"Dad, these are my friends from St. Augustus." There was an edge to Cole's voice.

"I'm the one who got attacked," said Ethan, grinning as he stuck out his hand. "But I'm fine, no harm done."

"You're the student?" Mr. Coffman took a step back as though Ethan's hand were Izzy himself, poised to strike.

"He's not a scary owl," Ethan said, dropping his hand. "It was a misunderstanding."

"Are you all right?" Brenda rushed over to Ethan, putting her protective mother arms around him. "Cole, you didn't tell me that."

Ethan's cheeks flushed a deep crimson at the sudden attention.

"It's the first I'm hearing about an owl attack." Cole's arms were folded across his chest.

So much for keeping him out of this.

"How do you know about the owl in the woods?" Ava asked Mr. Coffman.

"When you've lived in a town as long as we have, you hear stories." He chuckled.

"What stories?" Ava asked, echoing my thoughts.

"None with any merit, of course," he said, backpedaling as he pulled at his brown beard.

"Ava, maybe we'd better go..." Ethan said. He placed his hand on the doorknob.

"You kids haven't even had your hot chocolate yet! Cole, you haven't been a very attentive host," Brenda scolded. "Are you done with the house papers? If you are, I can bring your drinks to the dining room."

"House papers, what house papers?" Mr. Coffman still hadn't taken off his coat and shoes. He stood in a puddle on the hardwood floor, left by snow melting from his rubber overshoes. He gave us a tight smile.

"We're looking for information on an M. Hastings, who we think lived here in the twenties," I said.

This conversation was going in circles. There was no Hastings here. He'd confirm this and Ava and Ethan would be on their way. Ethan's owl attack was no reason to postpone our walk.

Mr. Coffman's smile fell, sending a chill up my spine. His eyes narrowed.

"There was a family here then. Henry and Matilda Jackman. They both died young, but they had a daughter who lived in the house until she got married in 1940 and moved away." He didn't need to look at the papers Cole showed us. He knew the history cold. "Matilda Jackman's maiden name was Hastings. She married

Henry in 1920."

I drew in a sharp breath. It wasn't a dead end and Isaac Young's lover had married someone else, who'd raised her daughter. The silence in the foyer unnerved me. It was like we'd just uncovered a scandal that would rock the headlines, instead of an almost hundred-year-old affair.

The thing was, Cole's parents were just as rattled as we were. Brenda wrung her hands and Mr. Coffman had gone quiet. Cole had said the West Woods riled his parents up. Why was that?

After a stretched-out pause, Brenda spoke. "Is this for a school project?"

"Not exactly. We're trying to stop the road development through the West Woods," Ava said. "Matilda's name came up and we followed a hunch."

"Oh?" Brenda asked.

The awkward silence in the foyer spread deeper. She and her husband exchanged wary looks.

"Courtney, are you still up for that walk?" Cole asked, stretching for Husk's leash.

Husk's bark gave me a start.

"Yes," I said. I wasn't sure what was happening, but the conversation about Matilda Hastings was over.

"Thanks for coming, guys," Cole said to Ava and Ethan. "We'll walk you to the main road."

I hadn't seen Cole take charge like this before. He handed me my hat and coat then snapped Husk's leash onto his collar. Husk's claws clacked on the wood floor as he hopped around, his body much too big for the crowded foyer. Cole opened the front door and led us out, Husk leading the way.

Mrs. Coffman waved from the warmth of the doorway then recovered her voice. "Nice to meet you all," she called.

"Thanks for having us." I waved, smiling until my teeth hurt from the cold. I shrank into my jacket to find warmth. I'd made a terrible impression on Cole's parents but they'd been very distracted. Maybe they hadn't noticed my behavior.

As soon as the door closed, Ethan rounded on Cole. "What was that about?" he asked.

Ava rubbed Husk's fur as he bounded happily around her, thumping the snow on either side of the shoveled sidewalk with his strong tail.

"Your dad didn't seem happy that we were asking about the house," Ethan said.

"Oh, he doesn't mind talking about the house," Cole said, trudging forward while shortening Husk's leash. "He could talk about our house all day. It's having a conversation about the woods I want to avoid. My dad works for the city planning committee. It's how I got the job there."

His hand was white under the pressure of Husk's leash. Husk ran in place in front of the next yard.

"He thinks the woods are too wild to be in the city limits and wants them gone," Cole said.

"He doesn't want the animals?" I asked.

I'd only seen birds and Izzy in the woods. Why would anyone want to drive out animals? Cole couldn't feel the same way, could he?

"I'm not defending him." Cole let out a long breath. "He likes animals fine. Well, maybe not owls. You heard him. Dad gets crazy about the woods. He could talk all day about our house, but he could spend the rest of his life talking about the woods."

"Why does he hate the woods?" Ava asked, looking back down the block at Cole's house. "Maybe whatever he knows would help."

Mr. Coffman's reaction had been odd, I agreed with her. I wanted to know too but I bit my tongue.

"Trust me, I was doing you a favor by not letting him talk," Cole said. "Once he gets started, there's no stopping him. He wants the road to go through the woods. The road will make access to the interstate safer and faster."

"Wasn't it supposed to go on the other side of town?" Ethan asked.

"It was," Cole said. "But the other proposed site is worse. It reroutes traffic to the eastern outskirts of Evergreen, and local businesses are worried it will affect them."

I frowned. "Well that doesn't sound good."

"There has to be another option," Ava said, pulling her unbuttoned coat together in the front.

I shrugged. "Maybe we just don't have all the information."

Ava sent knives my way with her eyes, as though she'd thrown a dozen at once. My shoulders sagged, curling in. Even if our goals were different, I cared what she thought. It would be nice to have a friend. One who knew me at my worst. One who forgave me.

"Do you agree with your dad?" Ava asked Cole.

"I think the road will be too close to the school." Cole kicked a pebble on the sidewalk with his foot. "There has to be another way. I'd like to help with the carnival. That is, if Courtney wants me to help."

My eyebrows shot up and my hands flew to my hips. "Of course," I said. My voice was shaky, like my wavering nerves. Of course, I wanted him there.

"I wouldn't miss it." He smiled broadly and took my hand. "Now if you can see yourselves back to campus, Courtney and I are going for a walk."

My hand tingled with his warmth.

"And Husk." Ethan laughed.

Husk barked at the mention of his name and came to us, licking our hands where they were joined. Things were going well with the second chance I'd been given, but I'd still be more comfortable if everything I'd done were erased.

CHAPTER TWELVE

Ava

"I haven't told Margaret she's not swimming. I need to tell her," I said.

Ethan and I sat in the cafeteria the next morning at breakfast. When I'd given Coach Laurel my decision, that Courtney would swim for the Owls, I asked if I could tell Margaret myself. I thought if it came from me it would be less hurtful but I was second guessing that.

"Margaret won't mind, you said." Ethan dug into his cereal.

Was he even listening? I *had* said that, although I didn't believe it. We had swim practice that afternoon. She'd find out then, whether I told her or not.

"Maybe she can just find out from Coach Laurel," I said. My chest fluttered as I spotted Margaret and Courtney at a far table. Their heads were bent low, discussing something. I'd planned to say it was temporary but she wasn't blind. Courtney was faster, a lot faster than Margaret. If she were allowed to swim, Margaret wouldn't be coming back this season. Or next.

"You saw the stone at Cole's, right?" he said.

I blinked at his abrupt change in subject. I took a deep breath, trying to let go of the bad news I had to deliver to Margaret and focus on what Ethan was saying.

"It's all connected," Ethan added.

The search for M. Hastings at Cole's house the night before

had turned up the first name Matilda. Despite our efforts to find out more, she was either too old or too dead to have an internet presence. We hadn't found a single lead online. Cole was going to search the town's records to see if there was anything else.

"There's no way it's a coincidence. His rock looked just like mine." He rolled the rock he'd taken from Ms. Krick around in his palm.

"Put that away," I said, curling my hand around his to make a fist. "The last thing we need is for Izzy to come flying in here right now." My eyes flitted to the exits, where I expected him to swoop in at any moment.

"Izzy's gone, remember?" Ethan frowned. "I'm afraid he's not coming back."

"What are you afraid of?" Jules asked, sliding into the seat next to me and pulling her kilt down over her thighs. "I hope you're not afraid of being a judge at the carnival?" Jules' comment came from left-field.

"A judge?" I asked, as Ethan smirked.

"If I'm part of the judging, I can't be named carnival queen," Jules said, simply.

"You'll make a lovely ice queen, Jules." Ethan snickered.

"Is ice king a thing?" Jake sidled up to our table, shaking his blond locks with dramatic flair and tossing his tray on the table. The four hard-boiled eggs he'd chosen for breakfast slipped around in their bowl with the movement.

"We might be losing focus a little," I said. Naming a carnival king and queen wouldn't save the fountain. "The important thing is to rally the community around saving the woods."

"We don't want the highway coming through here." Jules shrugged. "But we can have some fun trying to stop it, can't we?"

"Of course, we care about the woods getting wrecked. We'll miss all those nice trees to hug, even if we're never allowed near them," Jake said.

I shot him knives with my eyes. Why was he even helping with the carnival?

"I think the contest will help get students out to the park. It can't just be stuffy speeches." Jules' lower lip protruded.

"The town isn't going to listen to a bunch of students, led by a lunatic old teacher." Jake peeled the shell off an egg in two large pieces, which he discarded on the tray. "Might as well have fun."

Ethan was no help. He still had his rock and placed it on his forehead with his head tipped back. He balanced it while moving his head from side to side.

"So, will you do it?" Jules asked me. She always had just the right amount of sparkle to her eye shadow.

I should have been insulted that she thought I had no chance at being named queen, but I wasn't. I wouldn't be caught dead standing in front of the town in a robe and crown, with all their eyes on me, judging. And, running the contest would get me out of organizing the rentals, where I'd be stuck with a counter full of smelly skates for the whole event. Ethan and I needed to be free to talk to Senator Wallis, to the mayor, to anyone who would listen.

"I'll do it if we can name the king and queen right at the start," I said. I'd get my job out of the way early then I could mingle.

Jules pouted. "Is that even possible? Don't you have to count the votes and everything?"

"If we're crowned early, we'll be king and queen for the whole party, right?" Jake asked, leaning in.

"I guess so," I said.

Jules and Jake spoke as if their crowns were a done deal, like there was no competition. I caught Ethan's eye roll.

"I'd love to be queen for the whole event." Jules was practically drooling. "We can borrow robes from the drama club from last year's Shakespeare production. And I think there are crowns too. Will there be dancing?"

Her toothy grin lit up.

"You know she'll kill you if she doesn't win," Ethan said to me from the side of his mouth.

"Jules knows I won't play favorites." I hoped that was true.

Jules laughed. She'd heard us. "Maybe I shouldn't have asked the most honest person I know to run the carnival queen vote," Jules said. "Luckily, we won't need to cheat. We plan to win it fair and square."

I stared at Jules, whose dimples on her tanned cheeks would melt any heart. She genuinely loved parties. Events were her thing and she enjoyed planning them as much as being the life of the party. However, I didn't feel like an honest person these days and her saying it made me cringe. The secrets layered inside me could fill a room. They stifled me.

"Good morning," Margaret said. "Can I sit with you guys?"

I exchanged a look with Ethan. Margaret didn't sit with us often. She must have something on her mind. Maybe she'd suggest Courtney should take her spot on the team. That was the kind of thing she did all the time. I'd be off the hook if that was the case.

"Sure," I replied, scooting over to make room on the bench next to me.

I should just get it over with. If someone told me I wasn't going to compete in the pool for the rest of the year, it would crush me but Margaret was different.

"Courtney is going to swim in our next meet." There. I said it.

"Great," she answered, tucking into her bowl of Rice Krispies, which crackled in its milk with a snap, crackle, and pop. "We could use her. And that's actually what I wanted to talk to you about."

I breathed a sigh of relief.

"I was worried you weren't going to give her a chance. I got the feeling you don't like her. I'm glad I was wrong." Margaret's brow furrowed.

The table went silent, with all eyes on me.

"I-I like her," I stammered. I was genuinely trying to like Courtney. "And I'm glad you don't mind being an alternate. At least for now."

"Oh." Margaret's smile fell and my stomach plummeted with it.

I'd been too subtle. She hadn't grasped what I'd said, that Courtney would bump her. Jules patted Margaret's arm, as Margaret stared into her cereal.

"I'm sorry," I whispered. It wasn't enough. I should have at least told her privately. What was I thinking? I reached for her shoulder, but she shrugged it away.

"That's okay," she said.

"So, who do we think is going to challenge Jules for the title of carnival queen?" Ethan asked.

I thanked him silently for changing the subject.

"Excuse me," I mumbled, pushing myself to a standing position.

Margaret's miserable silence was too much for me. She'd stopped eating and poked around the soggy cereal in her bowl with her spoon. I'd talk to her later and smooth things over. After I got some air.

Ethan hurried behind me as I strode to the foyer.

"Bold move to tell her in front of everyone," he said, with no admiration in his voice.

"I know."

She'd caught me off guard sitting with us. I wasn't on my game. I had no business being team captain. I'd just hurt one of the nicest girls on our team. She may not win many meets, but she supported everyone with her positivity. She'd sat with me at breakfast to advocate for Courtney, who she'd just met. She had more right to be captain than me.

"I'm a little preoccupied." I pushed open the heavy metal door to the outside and stepped out, breathing deeply.

"You don't have a jacket," Ethan said, sounding like my dad for a moment. "It's cold."

In Massachusetts you couldn't go anywhere without a jacket. I'd momentarily forgotten. I didn't answer, instead leaning against him, letting him put an arm around me. The moist morning air filled my lungs with cold.

"What's going on over there?" said Ethan. He pointed across the lawn to the street, where two white vans were parked in front of the woods, while a third sat in the middle of the path at the edge of the campus lawn. *Animal Control* was emblazoned on the side of all three vans in a crimson, serious typeface. People in white jumpsuits weaved in and out of the trees, the men's and women's necks craned upward. The rest of the campus was quiet. There was still ten minutes until students would make their way to class.

"They're still looking for Izzy," I said, noting that there were more of them than the day before.

Ethan shook his head. "This is getting ridiculous. How many resources are they throwing at this?"

"Cole's dad won't rest until he's found." My stomach churned. I'd grown to like Izzy.

"They won't find him," Ethan said, his voice sure. "He'll stay out of sight. I tried to call him with my stone earlier this morning and he didn't come."

"You did?" How early had he been up that morning? And I noticed he called the stone *his*. He wasn't planning to give it back to Ms. Krick.

"Yeah, I wanted to warn him, but I think he already knows," he said. "He won't come back until the heat's off, I expect."

He spoke about Izzy as if he were a person. In some ways I thought of him like that too.

I squinted at the trees. There was another, smaller figure out there, moving quickly between the tree trunks. "Is that Ms. Krick?" I asked.

A broad smile of recognition broke out on Ethan's face.

"She'll make sure they don't find him, if he's still around. Won't she?" I asked.

"She will," Ethan said, relaxing his shoulders.

A beat passed between us. I pictured Izzy's bright eyes, watching us, almost like he could read our thoughts. I shivered.

"What do you think Izzy is?" I asked.

He was unusually smart. Were all owls like that? He was the first one I'd ever seen up close. We talked to him like it was the most natural thing in the world and he'd responded. Ethan's scrapes from Izzy's panic had mostly healed over. They were shallow.

"He lives in the woods with the fountain," Ethan said. He stopped walking. "I think he might be enchanted by it."

He stood in front of me, palms out. His explanation was absurd but not as absurd as what I was about to say. Why would a student wish for an owl to act like a human? I shook my head.

"His name is Izzy," I whispered. What I was about to say might be off the deep end. Ethan was going to laugh, but I couldn't shake it. Izzy had all the answers we'd been looking for and he was being hunted. Ms. Krick talked to him like an old friend. Cole's dad had a vendetta going back many years. Once I said it, I couldn't take it back. Yet the shiver rippling over my bones told me I was right.

"I think he's the spirit of Isaac Young."

Ethan didn't laugh. Instead, he nodded. He agreed.

CHAPTER THIRTEEN

Ava

Margaret was already in the pool when I arrived to swim practice that night after supper, her swim cap bobbing in and out of the water with every stroke. She was often the first one in, the hardest working.

I winced each time Margaret's arms sliced through the water, sending splashes into the lane next to her. She wasted so much energy with her strokes. If she were more efficient with her efforts, she could be a terrific swimmer, or at least there was that potential. Then I wouldn't be bumping her from the team.

"Ava, I have the roster here for the Boston meet." I hadn't seen Coach Laurel join me on the deck. She handed me a clipboard. "It needs your signature," she added.

"Sure." I was wet from my cleansing shower and my knees shivered as I took the clipboard. I read it over twice.

She'd made a mistake.

"Coach, Courtney should be the swimmer and Margaret the alternate." I pointed at Margaret's name, listed as the last registered swimmer. Courtney was a footnote on the page. Our alternate.

"No mistake. Didn't Courtney speak to you about it?" Coach frowned. "She came to me earlier today. She didn't feel Margaret should lose her place. She insisted on being our alternate for the rest of the year. We'll give her a permanent spot next fall."

A hot rush pushed into my temples. Courtney had done this behind my back, after I'd embarrassed Margaret at breakfast. I'd been so sure the right thing to do was to give Courtney her rightful spot. The spot she had... before. I opened and shut my mouth, nothing coming out. I should have fought harder for Margaret. Courtney had done the right thing. And I had not.

"Ava, I had left the decision to you." Coach Laurel watched me carefully. "But I was frankly surprised at your plan to replace Margaret. She's a member of our team. I think this arrangement is best."

So, it was done. Margaret had been upset and I'd done that. Coach was giving me an out, a way to fix one small wrong I'd done.

"Yes, of course," I said. I signed the roster the team would submit, scribbling my name in blue ink at the bottom. At the far end of the pool, Courtney hopped into Margaret's lane and stopped her mid-stroke. After a brief exchange between the two while they treaded water, Courtney proceeded to demonstrate the arm placement that would reduce Margaret's splash with drawn out, slow motion strokes. Why hadn't I gone and done that?

Margaret mimicked her motions, reducing her splash by at least half. After a few strokes, Margaret grabbed the wall at the end of the pool and the two girls shared a laugh. It was nice to see Margaret smile. I hoped she'd forgive me.

I watched them for a long moment as Coach Laurel collected the clipboard from my grasp and left me standing alone on the pool deck. Helping teammates was an important trait in a captain. Maybe it was the most important trait. It was one that *this* Courtney had in spades.

"We've got to try calling Izzy again." Ethan flipped the blue stone in his hand. He'd gotten adept at letting it roll along the top of his pale knuckles in a rippling pattern. He'd met me after practice at the sports complex to walk me back to the girls' dorm. There were only fifteen minutes until curfew, not enough time to go anywhere. I shifted my weight on the dorm steps. Ethan wasn't allowed to come in.

I shook my head. "You'd be calling him to his death." Two of the white vans had gone, but one was still parked at the side of the road, waiting. "Besides, I don't think he'd come. Your rock hasn't glowed since he left."

"They want to catch him, not kill him," Ethan said. "But we won't let him get caught. They can't stay all night."

"You can't stay all night either," I reminded him. My feet were cold. I wiggled my toes, which had lost feeling. "And Izzy's given us the pages. If he has anything else, he'll find us."

We hadn't asked Izzy to help. He just had.

"There has to be something else we can do." Ethan put the stone back in his pocket. "Every day that passes the construction plans will get firmer."

"We're doing it," I said. "The carnival." My shoulders sagged. The event was turning into, well, a carnival. With music, dancing, skating, and kings and queens. Awareness of the woods and the road had been sidelined.

"That's not going to work." Ethan's eyes darkened.

"Cole works in the city planning office. Maybe he could help us find a loophole in their permits," I said, grasping for something, anything else.

Ethan frowned. "He said he only files papers, but you could be onto something. Do we know anyone in construction planning?"

I slapped my forehead. I was still getting used to the timeline we lived in. "I can't believe I haven't talked to my dad," I said.

Construction planning, or roads or something, was exactly what Dad did now. Or at least since I'd wished Courtney's family away. I still thought of him as an engineer, working in an office.

"Do you think he'll help?" Ethan asked.

"If we explain, then yes." I swallowed hard.

"Did you tell him about your wish?" He cast a look over his shoulder at the silent campus lawn. Everyone was inside already. Warm. Getting ready for bed.

"No, but he made a wish, too, remember?" I said.

When I'd been home at Christmas, I'd avoided all talk of the fountain. I didn't want to think about Dad wishing for my mother's love.

"Do you think your dad ever found the fountain?" I asked, changing the subject.

"I don't know if he made a wish when he was here and I don't really want to. The whole thing gives me the creeps," Ethan said, shuddering.

His dismissal of the fountain stung. How could he want to be in the dark?

"We already know your dad's wish, so you should definitely talk to him about it," he said. "We need all the help we can get."

"I'll call him from my room," I said.

It was late. My heart raced. My phone buzzed the curfew alarm in my pocket. If I didn't go in now, I'd have detention for the rest of the week and there was too much to do.

"I should go." Ethan's smile was tight. "Text me when he answers to let me know what he says." He pecked me on the cheek, and raced down the steps.

I placed my hand on my cheek where his lips had brushed me. His shadow disappeared behind the main building, the path to the boys' dorm. When would we have time for more than a fleeting kiss?

A banging sound from above alerted me to Jules at our window. Her hair was in a top knot, as it was every night before bed. She waved with quick strokes for me to come in and I obeyed.

"When will our time be ours again?" Ethan asked, distracted as his fingers traced the length of my cardigan sleeve.

We'd invited every alumni kid to gather in the lounge the next day after school. It was Dad's idea and a good one. Two dozen alumni kids had come and they squirmed restlessly in their seats around the sprawl of low tables in the lounge. We'd inconvenienced them. Their parents had all gone to the school. Some of these kids must know about the fountain. If we could find only a few, and impress on them the importance of saving it...

"If we don't save the fountain, you won't have any time left at all." I brushed Ethan's hand off my arm gently. We were being watched.

"Touché," he replied. "I'll follow your lead."

I cleared my throat. Ethan was the one who was comfortable speaking in front of crowds, not me.

"What's this about?" asked Lily, a senior, as she stood at the back of the gathering with her arms crossed.

My stomach fluttered. They were waiting for me to speak. I squared my shoulders and leaned against one of the chair backs. Ethan's smile gave me strength.

"As most of you know," I began. "The West Woods is going to be flattened to make way for a highway as soon as the ground thaws." Blood rushed in a flush up my neck as I spoke. I stood before a sea of blank faces. They didn't care about the road. None of them had come to Krick's meeting about the woods. None had joined the carnival planning committee. I had to make them care.

"Your families are alumni of the school. They have a stake in the woods as well. We're asking you to invite your parents to the carnival this Saturday, to get involved with the fight against the road." My words went over like a flat pancake landing on their heads. A pair of freshmen boys at the back wandered away, tossing a football between them.

"I'll help," said Ruby, a girl in our year who I didn't know well waved her hand in the air. "What do you need?"

I smiled with gratitude at the lifeline she offered. "Just tell your parents what's happening and invite them on Saturday," I said. "Sign up here if you're willing to help."

I held up a sheet with a bunch of lines on it for them to add their details. The group was beginning to break up. Students turned their backs on me. Ethan stepped into the crowd and shoved pens into kids' hands, ushering them to the sign-up sheet. Four students formed a line in front of me.

"We're supposed to tell our parents to come to the carnival?" Marcus asked.

I blinked at his presence. I didn't know his family were alumni. Ethan had managed the invites to this meeting. So, we had at least one other alumni kid on the planning committee, besides Ethan, Courtney, and me. And Courtney's dad wasn't alumni in this timeline.

"Yes," I said.

"They live in Florida," he said. "But I'll tell them about it."

A heavy burden pressed on my chest. Florida? On short notice? They wouldn't be able to come.

Ethan waded through the kids that were still there, talking to each of them.

"We didn't get many names," I said, once my line had cleared.

"On the contrary," Ethan said, holding up his notebook, open to a page where signatures were scrawled on every line. "I got them all to promise to tell their parents."

I smiled. Sometimes he was brilliant. "Good, you got phone numbers," I said. "My dad wants to call them."

That had been his idea as well. I hugged Ethan's notebook to my chest and he put his arms around me. We were getting the word out. We needed every alumni family to help.

My kilt swished at my knees as I crossed the cafeteria. Courtney and Margaret laughed together about something as I passed the table they sat at. Heat flashed up my neck. What if they were laughing at me? They'd overturned my decision to let Courtney swim. I gave my head a shake. I was being petty. They most likely weren't laughing at me. I couldn't lose sight of the bigger picture. Shaking off my trepidation, I squared my shoulders.

"Courtney?" This conversation had been a long time coming. If I was ever going to accept this new Courtney into my life, we needed to clear the air. "Can we talk?"

CHAPTER FOURTEEN

Courtney

Ava ambushed me at breakfast. She stood by our table, her arms crossed, insisting we talk. She didn't have to be so serious. I *wanted* to talk with her. I'd been trying to do just that all week. But somehow with her in front of me, her face so stern, I froze.

"I'm done eating," Margaret said. "You can have my seat." She swiped her tray in one motion from the table and stood without making eye contact with Ava. Margaret might be back on the swim team, but Ava hadn't handled the situation well and Margaret was going to need a minute to get over it.

Ava gave her a wide berth. She wrung her hands. Was she mad that I let Margaret keep her spot? I just couldn't take it from her. My ambition had gotten me into hot water before. I wasn't going to make the same mistake twice. I wasn't that person anymore. Again. Whatever.

"I should have told you I was going to turn down the spot," I said.

It was an apology of sorts. I'd practically begged Ava to let me swim. She had every right to be mad. She was team captain. The title wasn't mine, not anymore. I didn't want it. She could keep it.

Ava chewed her lower lip. Silence stretched between us. Was she waiting for me to speak? She was the one who'd asked to talk to me. My arms were crossed too. I'd done it without even noticing.

"I need to know what your wish was," she said.

"I'm glad we're talking," I said at the same moment, talking over her.

We both spoke at once then shared a laugh at our awkwardness.

"You first," I said.

If she was asking about wishes, she wasn't here on official team captain business.

Ava unclenched her fists at her sides and took Margaret's vacant seat. She folded her hands in front of her on the table and took a deep breath. Finally, she made eye contact with me and I pushed down the urge to look away. There was deep strength in her. I admired her strength, but it also unnerved me.

"I need to know more about your wish." Her voice cracked a little.

I took a deep breath. "I wished to complete a list." Tears pricked at my eyes as I remembered throwing the coin. It was a lifetime ago, a parallel lifetime even. I'd written a list of stuff I thought my parents wanted me to do. Things I thought if I completed, I could go home. The irony of it stung. In the present version of events, I'd pestered my parents until they let me come to St. Augustus. In my former life, when the school had been Dad's alma mater, I'd railed against it. I hadn't framed it that way in my mind until that moment.

"I pushed to become team captain because it was on the list. The fountain compelled me to do the things I did. At least I think it did... I thought once I checked everything off, I'd be free of it. Free to make my own decisions again, to be me. But I'd become someone else and I couldn't find my way back. I was horrible to Cole. And Violet. And especially you." My voice was only a whisper. Dredging this up hurt deep inside my chest.

"I think I remember Violet," Ava said, cocking her head to one side. "I met her on my first day at the dorm. Blond curls, right? I'd forgotten her until now. Is she still at the school?"

"No." I eyed her curiously. "She's been my friend since we were kids. Our parents spend a lot of time together. She went to St. Augustus with us before my life was reset, but she isn't here anymore."

Ava clapped her hand over her mouth. "Is she okay?" she whispered, the blood draining from her cheeks.

"Oh yes, she's fine," I said quickly. "She wears purple from head to toe every day and goes to a private school in Boston. I tried to convince her to come with me to St. Augustus, but she wasn't interested."

There was something freeing about telling Ava all of this. She was the one person who might understand. There was nobody else in the world I could talk to about it.

"That makes sense," she said. "It's because if she went to St. Augustus, you'd have heard of it."

"What?" I asked.

"My wish. I wished you and your family had never heard of St. Augustus," she said. "Violet couldn't be here. I did that." Her expression crumpled.

"Hey, I don't blame you," I said. "Violet's fine. I'm fine. I know I was horrid to you and you didn't deserve that. I'm sorry for all of it."

Ava studied the floor, her lips pursed.

"I was trapped," I continued. "I thought I was doing what I had to, to be free. It was *you* that freed me. Your wish..." My voice trailed off, as Ava pursed her lips.

"You made my second wish." I barely heard the words I spoke myself. I wanted only Ava to hear.

Her head jerked up. "You could still see the fountain, after your wish?" she asked, as her eyes narrowed. "Was it because you came back? Can you see the fountain now?"

I shook my head. "No. I went to the clearing, but the fountain wasn't there. It hasn't been there for me since my first wish. There was just the long grass." My whole body shook as I remembered the things I'd done. "I tried to break the fountain's hold on me. I was in over my head. I felt like a completely different person, not myself." My judgment and actions had been affected by the fountain. I'd been horrible.

"How did you make a second wish?" asked Ava, impatience creeping into her words.

"I threw the coin into the grass where the fountain should be." I arched my arm overhand, mimicking throwing a coin. "And I wished that my family and I had never heard of St. Augustus."

All the blood drained from Ava's face. Her eyes went wide and her jaw dropped.

"Ava?" I rushed over to prop her up where she listed to one side. "Are you all right?"

CHAPTER FIFTEEN

Ava

The Saturday of the carnival rushed toward us with the speed of a Mack truck on the freeway, trying to make up time, although if the carnival did its job, that freeway wouldn't run through the St. Augustus campus.

My calendar was full of details. Every minute of my time until the guests arrived was planned. We'd commandeered a corner of Ms. Krick's classroom, where large jars and several buckets of silver pebbles were stacked, ready for the coronation vote. Streamers and banners were heaped in a pile.

"You're going to make *me* the carnival king, right?" Ethan said to me, as he reached into one of the buckets and pulled out the stone. He ran his thumb over it, frowning.

I laughed. "Stop, you're as bad as Jules," I said.

Ethan would look wonderful in the king's robe we'd borrowed from the drama room above the stage. The robe was deep blue, with white trim and a fur collar. If he wanted to be king, he'd give Jake a run for his money. But he was kidding. Ethan didn't need the recognition. He commanded any room he was in and didn't need a title to do it.

Jules and Jake, on the other hand, had been talking to anyone who'd listen about their campaign. There wasn't a student on campus that didn't know their names were in the running. Jules bragged about her plans to make the winter carnival an annual event and how she'd be pleased as their queen to organize skating events through the rest of the term. They were shoo-ins.

Dad had arrived late the night before and headed straight to Gran's. He'd rented a van to help us set up in the park.

"Dad will be here soon. Let's bring as much down as we can," I said.

Ethan filled his arms with picket-style Bristol board signs with bright letters. We'd painted STOP THE ROAD and SAVE THE WEST WOODS. They weren't going to be enough. I shivered. When we'd made them, I was tempted to paint SAVE ME FROM BEING ERASED FROM HISTORY.

Jules hadn't helped with the signs. "They'll cheapen the event," she said.

"They're the whole point of the event," I replied, ending the debate. We had to keep focus.

My phone buzzed. It was Dad, texting that he was out front. "Let's go," I said.

"Are you going to introduce me to your dad as your boyfriend?" Ethan asked, peering over the signs he carried. The blush on his cheeks made my heart clench.

"Do you want me to?" I asked. Did I want to? Ethan and I had worked together on the carnival but there was still a distance between us that we hadn't talked about. The timing hadn't been right. He knew me better than Lucas ever had, didn't he? Still, I hesitated. I wasn't sure my heart was ready.

"Yes," Ethan said, the signs he held slipping lower in his grip.

"Here, let me help you." I took a few signs off the top, lightening his load.

Dad had tried to talk me out of breaking up with Lucas over the Christmas break, asking me to consider giving Lucas more time. He said not to do anything rash. But I'd known dragging out what needed to be done wasn't right. Time wasn't the problem.

My relationship with Lucas had been comfortable. There was love. Then when everything happened with the fountain, it hit me like a ton of bricks. Lucas wasn't the person I turned to. He would never have believed me if I had. Everything about him was practical and we wanted different things. Anything he couldn't see or touch didn't exist and I couldn't explain that to Dad. Or at least it had felt that way.

I hadn't told Dad I'd been hanging out with Ethan. It hadn't seemed important.

But Ethan had listened. He'd been open. He saw my heart, even if it wasn't quite ready to fall, again.

"Then I will," I said. I slung two reusable shopping bags, brimming with decorations, over my shoulder. My arms were full of signs. We'd have to make several trips.

"This past month has been confusing," Ethan said, pausing on the threshold of the classroom.

"I know." If there hadn't been a good time before to hash this out, now was worse. My phone buzzed in my pocket. Dad would be wondering where we were. "And I'm sorry."

Ethan's dark eyebrows shot up. I realized after it came out of my mouth what it sounded like. It sounded like a goodbye.

"No, no!" I said, in a rush. "I love spending time with you. I don't know what I'd do without you. I *want* to be your girlfriend. I've just been distracted..."

Ethan leaned in for a kiss but our arms were still full. He awkwardly managed to plant a dry kiss on my cheek without his pile of signs squirting out of his arms. We both laughed.

"Your dad's waiting," he said.

I loved Ethan's smile. It chased away the darkness huddled inside me.

We could work on this, build something that would last.

"So, Ethan Roth?" Dad chuckled as he pulled the full van away from the curb. I'd asked Ethan to meet us over at the park after lunch. Dad had shaken Ethan's hand without saying much when I'd introduced them. The word "boyfriend" had stuck in my throat. I'd introduced him as a friend, but the tremor in my voice was enough to give me away.

"He's been a good friend," I said.

The van had that new car smell, of tire rubber and upholstery cleaner. I hated it. I fidgeted with my hands in my lap. We were headed to Luigi's for brunch.

"His father's a good sort." Dad's mouth twitched at the corner.

He was trying not to laugh. I was dating the son of his friend. His friend that Mom had dated before she started dating Dad, before his wish. It was all very complicated.

"I'm glad you find this amusing." I folded my arms. Dad was enjoying this a little too much. Wasn't talking about boyfriends with daughters supposed to be uncomfortable for the parent? I was the one squirming.

"He seems like a nice kid and I trust your judgement, Ava," Dad said, as he slowed the van down, flashing me a look. "But we have to save the woods."

"Yes." It was hard for me to catch Dad's eye while he drove, but it was as good as an admission. He'd come to the same conclusion about the fountain that we had. "And Ethan's helping with that."

"As well he should," he said. "He's at risk too." Dad turned the steering wheel, hand over hand, pulling the van to the curb on a street lined with houses.

My pulse quickened. Ethan and I had discovered Dad's wish and guessed at the implications. Still, hearing him confirm it was unsettling.

Dad turned in his seat, his seatbelt still done up and straining against his shoulder as he leaned toward me. "Did you make a wish?"

His question was simple. But my answer wasn't. We'd never discussed the fountain. What I'd done had affected him as much as anyone. This was going to come as a shock. I shuddered in a breath, digging deep. I found the smallest kernel of bravery in my core and nurtured it, coaxing it out.

"I wished a girl, Senator Wallis' daughter, Courtney, would disappear and then she did. And Dad, I'm so sorry..." Tears burned behind my blinking eyelids. I'd cost Dad his job. Our home.

Dad frowned. "I'm not sure I know a Senator Wallis."

"You did."

He had. Senator Wallis had helped Dad graduate from St. Augustus. Without Courtney's dad, mine wouldn't have passed the twelfth grade. In this timeline, he hadn't. Keeping it all straight made my head spin. But Dad's wish was the one keeping me up at night.

"Is the girl okay?" Dad asked, slowly.

"She's fine. She's actually back at St. Augustus, now. My wish only affected the past. She's helping us with the carnival." I crossed my arms. Voicing it out loud made my wish small, in the grand scheme. "But…"

"No harm done, then, right?" he said, as he let out a breath.

"It's you," my insides crumpled. We were talking about the fountain openly now. How was he going to react when he knew what I'd done?

"Me?" His eyes opened wide with surprise.

There was no way to cushion this. He'd been an engineer. I'd taken that from him.

"My wish screwed up your life." My words came out in a rush. Tears of anger filled my eyes. "You are supposed to be in Malaysia. You got a job there as an engineer. We had our own house." I clenched my teeth, bracing for the impact my words would have on him. "My wish took all that from you."

I wiped my cheek with my fist and lifted my gaze to look at Dad, who bent over from the waist, leaning on the steering wheel. Was he okay? His shoulders shook.

My jaw hung open. Of all the reactions I'd imagined when I told him what I'd done, this was the last thing I expected. He was laughing.

"Dad?" I put my hand on his shoulder.

"Sounds like you saved me from a pretty boring life." He let a loud snort rip, then erupted in a fresh peal of laughter, slapping the steering wheel.

I sat back, flummoxed. I hadn't heard my Dad's soul-touching belly laugh since Mom died.

"Where are your skates?" Ethan called to me. He raced around the freshly shoveled pond at the park, skating after Jake. The two were evenly matched, their blades scraping pale arcs into the ice.

Jake swiped at Ethan with his hockey glove, tagging his shoulder as Ethan flinched away. Ethan was good at every sport. He glided to the edge, hopping onto the bank, where his skates sunk into the wet snow.

"I was beginning to think you weren't coming. Where's your dad?"

"He's unloading," I said.

I'd left Courtney and Jules at the curb beside the van, unloading decorations. I'd told Dad about both of Courtney's wishes, about mine, about our worst fears if the fountain were destroyed. He hadn't reassured me. He couldn't. He'd agreed. My life depended on the past staying intact. Possibly Ethan's too.

The day of the carnival was the warmest we'd had in weeks, with the sun reflecting off the rink. Still, my hands were two blocks of ice. I had on my long winter coat, when everyone else had shed their outer layers, wearing only hoodies. Dads were supposed to be reassuring, but talking to mine had made me more on edge. A thin layer of snow glistened on the pond.

"The stage is almost ready," Ethan said, motioning to the rented black floor that spanned the far end of the park. A rack of lights stretched ten feet above its platform and several speakers lined the edges.

"Are you giving up?" Jake called to Ethan. He stopped beside us on the bank with his two skates parallel. He lurched abruptly, spraying snow on Ethan's jeans but missing me.

"Hey!" Ethan brushed Jake's assault off his pants and pulled his boots out from under a green-painted bench. He sat heavily down beside two snow shovels leaning on the edge of the seat. "Quitting while I'm ahead," Ethan called back, as Jake feigned offence by clutching his chest and skating away.

Hockey wasn't popular in California. I'd been on skates only a few times.

Ethan looked right at home. He pulled off his right skate. "It took us a while to shovel the snow. Just having a little fun."

"I told my dad everything." I sat on the bench next to him, digging my hands into the pockets of my coat.

"And?" Ethan put his socked feet on top of his skates, off the snow. He stopped to look at me.

"He thought my wish was hilarious," I admitted.

"What?" His brow crinkled.

"He said he never wanted to be an engineer." This information was still fresh. I was trying to assimilate it. "And he loves living with Chuck and Mia. He can afford a house. He's been able to for a while. He's happy."

"Huh," was all Ethan said.

"When I brought up his wish, his face went dark," I said.

He'd manufactured his relationship with my mom. Their marriage. Me. It was all at risk. Dad shared our fears. If the woods were flattened, it could all be undone.

"Does he have any ideas to help us fight?" Ethan asked.

"He's been working on it since I first called him," I said. "He's meeting with the crew today that drew up the highway plans. He's going to their job site in town right after we unload the van." I waved an arm at Dad, who loaded blue plastic bins onto the sidewalk. Courtney and Jules ferried them to stations set up through the park.

"If the deal with Valentine can be overturned, he'll figure out how," I said. "He's worried."

"Me too," Ethan said, pulling on his boots and offering me a hand up.

"Everything's out of the van," Jules said as we neared the curb.

Bins were stacked on the sidewalk. She closed the hatch to the trunk by tugging down and letting it swing shut. Jules had tucked her jeans into the fur cuff of her black boots and she wore a woolly beige sweater with matching scarf, mitts, and beanie. She'd picked out an outfit of hers for me to wear too. It was still laid out on my bed at the dorm. Jules scrunched her nose at my dusty coat sleeves.

The van roared to life and Dad rolled down the passenger side window to wave as he pulled away. "I'll be back!" he called.

Whatever he could find out in town would help us more than setting up here.

Ethan and I each grabbed a bin. Mine could have been full of rocks it was so heavy. It said *Skate Rental*. Ethan's said *Stage*, so we split up.

At the far end of the pond a white trailer was parked behind an empty table. The trailer doors hung open. Shelving lined its interior walls, which were laden with pairs of rental skates. I smelled disinfectant as I approached. Tonight, our committee would provide volunteers to take money and hand out skates. I was glad I was handling the coronation vote and not sweaty skates.

A loud scratching noise came from deep inside the trailer. I dropped my bin on the empty table and circled back to investigate. Something scrabbled behind a thin metal door labeled "Storage" at the far end. I climbed up the retractable metal stairs into the bed of the trailer, listening. Sun from outside beat on my back, but my blood ran ice cold. Had an animal been trapped? I reached for the metal door, my hand shaking as the door to the closet flung open, banging against the metal trailer with its hinges screeching.

My heart leaped up into my throat.

"Ava, good." A heap of purple fur filled the doorway to the cramped room, dwarfing Ms. Krick's thin frame. "I need your help."

I stared at her violet faux-fur coat, which was matted. It was much too large, giving her the bulk of Barney the dinosaur. Her scrawny legs stuck out from under it and on her feet were a pair of well-worn figure skates, white with beige scuffs. Krick teetered on their blades, which were covered by a plastic sheath. I cleared my throat.

"My feet are extremely narrow." She waved a cellophane package in the air. "If I wear skates without cushioning, my heels will be covered in blisters. These foot pads will stop the chafing. Be a dear and help me?" She tossed the package in my direction.

I recoiled, backing away to the trailer opening, where there was more air. I didn't want to touch her feet. I let the package slap on the metal floor.

"Just shove those down the back of my skates." She picked up the package of padding and waved it at me, apparently unperturbed by my obvious distaste.

I scrambled backward down the stairs, catching my breath when my boots hit the snow. My mind had gotten the better of me and seeing Ms. Krick there made my heart skip several beats.

With the help of the black metal rail, Ms. Krick followed me, lowering herself to a seated position on the stairs.

"Are you going to skate?" I frowned at her feet. She was expecting blisters. Just how vigorously was she planning to skate?

A low chuckle escaped her throat, where her loose skin waggled under her chin. "Yes, but don't go spreading it around," she said. "I want my performance to be a surprise." She stroked her hair, which was pulled into its usual bun.

"Performance?" Resigning myself, I ripped open the cellophane package she handed me and fished out one of the peach-colored pads, its texture spongy, like white bread. "I thought you weren't allowed to organize the carnival?"

Ms. Krick smiled. "Performing is far from organizing. They can't stop me from skating and having a little fun." She thrust her foot at me. "Be sure to get it in far enough."

I stretched gingerly toward the back of her skate. I choked back a lump in my throat as I jammed the pad between the thin leather of the skate and her pantyhose-covered ankle, careful not to touch her.

"You'll have to wait and see, like the rest of them," she said.

There wasn't enough hand sanitizer in the world to make this okay.

"Maybe you just need a smaller skate?" I suggested. The pad had slipped easily down to the bottom of her heel.

"No, no, these are fine. They're perfect now," she said.

I held a second pad pinched between my fingers out to Ms. Krick, so that she could do it herself. I couldn't wait to wash my hands.

I smirked. Wait until Jules heard about Krick's addition to the evening program. Whatever it was, Jules wasn't going to approve of it being added.

"I'll let you in on another secret." Ms. Krick's wrinkles bunched up beside her eyes as she smiled. "A close relative of Isaac Young's will speak tonight."

"A relative?" I asked. "I didn't think he had any." My pulse quickened. If M. Hastings' daughter had kids, and any of them were still alive, they could be here, tracked down by Ms. Krick. We hadn't made any headway.

"Oh yes, he certainly does." She clapped her hands. "They will have to respect the history of the school once it all comes out."

"Is it someone related to M. Hastings?" I blurted without stopping to think if I should share what we knew. My heart raced. This might be just the break we needed.

"I always knew you were a smart one." Ms. Krick hauled herself to her feet by pulling on the railing then wagged a bony finger at me. "But you won't get me to talk."

She shuffled up the stairs and back into the trailer, leaving me standing in the snow. Sweat pooled at the nape of my neck. I'd finally warmed up. It was the perfect day for the carnival. We couldn't have asked for better weather. We should get lots of the townspeople out. I hoped our case was compelling enough to have them join our fight.

CHAPTER SIXTEEN

Courtney

I stood in the middle of the park, with a hundred feet of ribbon wrapped around my body like ten octopuses trying to hug me all at once. I spit out ribbon ends as they tried to worm their way into my mouth like tiny tongue lashes.

"You look like a Maypole," Cole said. He stomped snow from his runners, reaching to grab the bundle of ribbons.

"A winter Maypole? I've never heard of that." I tore at the endless tangles wound around me.

He laughed, pulling at my tormentors. "No! A *beautiful* Maypole."

The warm wind tickled my nostrils. I didn't feel beautiful. The whole park was strung with twinkle lights and streamers. I was supposed to hang strands of this ribbon from the trees, but I was hard pressed to find a corner of the park not already laden with festive charm. Jules' eye for detail was relentless. The result was a winter wonderland. Silver streamers hugged every tree. Each piece sparkled with the last light of the day, sending flashes into the dusky air.

Cole shook his head. "I've lived beside this park my whole life and I've never seen it look like this."

Jules and the others had gone back to the dorm to change. Cole had climbed up and down a ladder all afternoon while I threaded the decorations through my hands.

"It's magical," I said. I referred to more than just the trees. We'd laughed and talked easily all day. I was quickly falling for Cole.

He gently unraveled the strands of ribbon from my shoulders, letting them drop to the ground. "Let's just stuff this ribbon in the trash," he said. "Jules won't even notice it's missing."

I stuck out my tongue at him, which proved hard to do while smiling, but he was right. The park had been transformed. There was nothing more for us to do.

"The first guests are arriving already. I don't have time to go back and change." I sighed. A group of teens crossed onto the lawn, laughing together. I still had a few strands of ribbon tangled around my shoulders. I held my arms up to keep them from dragging on the ground.

"Those kids are from my school. The word's out. This carnival's definitely the most exciting thing to ever happen in Evergreen in January." Cole rummaged in the last bag of decorations we were supposed to put up and fished out a pair of shears. He deftly cut me free from the ribbons, rolling them into a tight ball.

"Those kids are seniors. And if they're coming, everyone's coming. You guys are going to make some noise. This just might work."

"Let's hope they bring their parents," I said. "Or better yet, the mayor."

Jules' version of carnival wasn't geared to attract either of those. Today had been great. If they somehow managed to save the woods, I could live with this do-over, I realized. Everything was falling into place.

"Er, yeah." Cole cleared his throat. "Let's just go to my house for a bit. My mom will feed us." He gave a small wave to the girls and boys congregating near the pond, but made no move to go over. Instead, he tipped my chin up to look at him. His freckles were a mirror of my own. His smile warmed through me.

"Courtney!"

The voice startled me, popping the bubble around us. It came from a dark sedan parked at the curb. Dad emerged from the back door. I pulled away from Cole, waving at the car.

"It's my dad," I said, taking Cole's hand and leading the way to meet him, our steps unhurried.

I was glad I wasn't able to dissuade Dad from coming. It had only been a few weeks, but memories of home came flooding back. He was here because I'd asked him to be.

We had to stop them from destroying the woods.

✧✧✧

An hour later, the park was filled. Cole had brought me a sandwich from his house, while I stayed with Dad. I was tired and my clothes were soiled from working in the park all day, but I didn't want to miss a minute of the carnival.

Dad was going to call out Valentine and the mayor in his speech, declaring that the property sale was "not in the town's best interest". His aides had given him several arguments to use and they were compelling.

City Hall had never called me back about the mayor speaking. Dad and Valentine were both on the program and I'd left it at that. I could have done more but I didn't. I hoped I'd done enough.

The lights over the stage snapped on shortly after we arrived, dousing Dad and me in a pool of light. The square black speakers suspended at either end of the stage thrummed to life with carnival music. Ms. Krick had provided the horrid soundtrack, despite being removed from our committee. Its cliché notes sent a shiver creeping up my spine. It conjured images of clowns and funhouses, not the winter wonderland we'd built. Jules better hurry up and get here. She definitely had something better planned.

The night was the warmest we'd had since I'd arrived in Evergreen. The townspeople and St. Augustus students were there in droves, lining up for the two food trucks on the street and the cotton candy machine that had appeared beside the pond. The rink was full of skaters, moving in a uniform circle around the perimeter of the ice.

Dad blew into the microphone, which echoed through the speakers over the music. It worked.

"I warned you not to get involved!" Headmistress Valentine's voice rose above the din in the park. She stood on the snow in front of the stage, waving her hands at Ms. Krick. "You shouldn't even be here."

The crowd withdrew into a circle around the women to watch the altercation, hiding smiles behind their hands. But their curiosity wouldn't be satisfied. Instead of yelling back, Ms. Krick turned on her heel and stormed away from the headmistress, stumbling a little on the ice. Her fluffy purple coat puffed up her back. She was a cross between a teddy bear and a monster, both fitting her duplicitous personality.

"What's she doing?" I said, under my breath.

"That was your last warning!" Headmistress Valentine yelled after her.

"Is everything all right?" Dad called out to Valentine from beside me on the stage, his voice booming through the speakers.

"Just fine, Senator Wallis." Valentine gave Dad a thin smile, turning quickly from him and pushing her way past a clump of students. She wasn't pleased that my dad was speaking out against the road, but she couldn't threaten to fire him like she had Ms. Krick.

"Are you sure you're okay with me calling out your principal?" Dad asked me in a low voice, covering the microphone.

I shrugged. "If it'll help," I said. I'd promised to help Ava and my Dad seemed to think he had the upper hand. My popularity with the headmistress was the last thing on my mind.

Dad nodded. He pulled out his cue cards where he'd scattered his notes for his speech. His lips moved as he read. He had this under control. I mumbled good luck and stumbled down the stage steps, where I was engulfed in a crush of students arriving to vote at the coronation station.

"I'll be the best carnival queen!" Jules pushed her way toward the foot of the stage, handing out neon blue buttons to everyone she passed, decorated with a Jules & Jake heart.

I blinked at her clothing, which looked more like a shiny superhero costume than an outfit for a carnival queen. Its striking blue fabric was tight and stretchy, hugging her curves and shimmering under the stage lights. She wore a jacket with plastic spikes shaped like icicles lining the lapel and tails hanging down her back to her knees. Her dark hair was plaited in a complex arrangement that framed her face like curtains and she wore a sequined mask over her eyes. She looked like a queen in a way only Jules could pull off.

Ava's voting booth was set up beside the stage, with several large glass jars on a long table. Ava stood at the end of the table, dressed all in silver, with a cape and a mask like Jules', only plainer. I laughed at her nonplussed expression. Why she'd agreed to let Jules dress her, I had no idea. She handed out silver pebbles to passers-by. Each pebble was a vote that they could drop into the jars on the table, for the king and queen of their choice. I didn't need to get any closer to know that Jules' jar was the one that was almost full. I smiled. She deserved it.

Under a tree peppered with twinkly lights, I spotted Cole.

He rushed over and grabbed my hand. "Can you skate?" Grinning, he led me to the rental trailer.

"Not well," I said, following him.

"Get your votes in right over there at our voting booth!" Ethan pointed at Ava's station from the stage. He spoke into the microphone. "The king and queen of our winter carnival will be announced shortly."

It was crowded by the pond. School hoodies from St. Augustus and Evergreen High in equal numbers looped around the pond in lazy circles under the bright lights. It was mostly guys chasing each other, but a few groups of girls skated together and there was the odd couple. There was even a toddler wearing snow pants with thick suspenders pushing a red metal walker around on her shaky skates.

"Size eleven," Cole said to the girl renting the skates. He smiled my way. "And what size do you need?"

"Six, men's. Hockey skates," I said.

"You play hockey?" he asked.

"I tried out for a team, once," I replied. I hadn't put in enough time to learn to skate well enough to make the team, between my commitments with running and swimming.

Cole nodded with appreciation.

I hugged my arms around myself, pleased to have impressed him. I loved every sport I'd ever tried. "Although I haven't skated in years," I added quickly, hoping skating was like riding a bike, and it would come back to me quickly.

The girl working at the skate trailer shrugged. "Sorry, we're out of most sizes right now," she said. "You'll have to wait." She waved her arm at a clump of students, standing off to the side of the trailer.

Cole frowned as I grabbed his arm. My skating legs didn't need to be tested.

"It's okay," I assured him. "They're going to announce the king and queen now anyway." And then my dad was going to speak. Butterflies in my stomach beat their wings as if I had to give the speech myself.

The music stopped, replaced by the laughter and din of the carnival. People were having fun. The speeches were going to be a downer.

"And the king and queen of Evergreen's first ever Winter Carnival..." Ethan's announcement was right on cue, resounding through the park on the speakers. "Jules and Jake!"

"They're your friends, right?" Cole asked, raising his voice above the cheers as he clapped politely.

"Yeah," I replied, grinning. There was no other possible outcome and yet, I was really happy for them.

Jules dragged Jake behind her onto the stage. He was dressed in shiny blue just like her, although his outfit was thankfully looser than her form fitting unitard. I couldn't help but laugh. He was a good sport. Ethan placed silver crowns on their heads with dramatic flair.

"Thank you so much!" Jules grabbed the microphone from Ethan's hands. "We're so honored to be here for the West Woods, who can't speak for themselves. Let's not forget what tonight is all about. There's a petition against building the road circulating in the park tonight. Make sure you sign it and let your voices be heard."

She and Jake took a bow. Jules held her crown tightly to her head with one hand, but Jake's toppled into the front row, sending a ripple of laughter through the audience. A tall girl in the crowd tossed it back at him like a football and he held his arms out to catch it. Of course, his practiced arms nailed it. The crowd roared their approval.

"Yes, yes. Congratulations to you both." Ms. Krick took the microphone from Jules in one swift movement. What was Krick doing on stage? She wasn't supposed to be part of the program. Her coat made her look twice as wide as she was. My dad was supposed to speak now. Was he not ready?

I craned my neck to see past the stairs leading to the stage. Where was Dad? Krick's words were terse and she shooed Jules and Jake from the stage with force.

"And now, it is my pleasure to introduce you to our guest of honor tonight, Massachusetts State Senator Wallis!"

A smattering of applause welcomed Dad to the stage, although instead of feeling relieved when he bounded up the stairs, my shoulders tensed. It was mostly students in attendance. They loved the crowning of the king and queen, but they weren't there to hear a politician.

Dad cleared his throat into the microphone as the crowd around the stage started to disperse. "Evergreen is rich with history and the legacy of St. Augustus and the woods are important," he began.

More students wandered away from the stage area. My heart dropped. Dad gave a nervous laugh, looking out over the crowd. "I don't want to bore you with a history lesson. I want to tell you that the way this road was approved was corrupt. It was thoughtless, greedy, and must be overturned. I'm here to tell you that I won't rest until a more appropriate place is found to build the road. One where your glorious football stadium won't be filled with car emissions. I'm officially opening an inquiry to make sure the decision makers here are made to pay for their careless actions."

The students had stopped. They were looking his way.

"I'm here to talk about the future, not the past." This was the Dad I'd heard talk to audiences since I was a child. Swaying opinions. Getting his way. "And to make sure that due process is restored in Evergreen's City Hall."

Every head in the park was turned his way. Dad paused for effect and the expected cheer came. The students had come for the carnival. But Dad, as always, knew his audience. I let out the breath I'd been holding. Dad had given them conspiracy theories. He said the leaders of the town were corrupt, that they'd made a mistake. These allegations were inflammatory. People were interested. They might make a difference.

I shook my head. He'd probably overstepped by saying these things, but maybe that's what we needed. Ava's signs were being handed out. Clipboards were being passed around the park. Krick's petition. Krick, who Headmistress Valentine had banned from helping, hadn't stopped planning from behind the scenes. I could see that now.

"We have letters of protest from a dozen alumni of St. Augustus across the country. Organized by alumni Steve Marshall, whose daughter, Ava, was instrumental in organizing today's event."

More applause. I searched the dense crowd for Ava. The letters of support were a surprise.

"This road is not going through without a fight." Dad raised his fist in the air and let the applause of the crowd shower him. The students were fired up.

"Your Dad's a great speaker," Cole said.

I nodded. My worry had fled. Dad delivered. He always did.

He waited for the clapping to die down, bowing his head in thanks. "And now, if we could clear the skaters from the pond," Dad said from the stage, gesturing in our direction. "I'm told there is to be a special presentation."

My head jerked up. What had he said? There wasn't another presenter. I hadn't invited anyone else, except the mayor, which had been a dead end.

Cole nudged me. "If the skaters leave the pond, they'll have to return their skates. Maybe they'll have our sizes."

"Yeah." I was less enthusiastic. My money was on Ms. Krick as the next speaker. The park was wall-to-wall people, which would easily hide a small teacher, even with her purple fur. I couldn't see her.

A loud thud came over the speakers and the stage's lights shone on a blank slate. The stage was empty. The first soft notes of a ballad wafted through the park.

"Is that your teacher?" Cole asked, pointing at the pond.

And it was. Ms. Krick stood at the top of the rink, tossing her oversized coat aside to reveal a skating costume even more hideous than the one she'd worn at the meeting in the gym. I slapped my forehead. What was she up to? Dad had gotten the crowd riled up, but she was about to make the whole event a laughing stock.

The bodice of her outfit was red and gold, with a much too short skirt hanging off her narrow hips. The whole ensemble shone with rows of sequins. She hopped down onto the pond wearing skates on her feet with a nimbleness that shouldn't be possible for someone her age.

"Come on, we have to stop her." I pushed my way through the people in front of me, motioning for Cole to follow. The soft music ended, and Ms. Krick stood in a ridiculous pose in the center of the pond, with one leg crossed over the other and her arms over her head. Laughter rippled all around us. I stopped short of stepping onto the ice. I shook my head. She couldn't really be going to skate?

A new song started, with a jazzy run of music. Ms. Krick pushed off on one foot as a mist billowed out over the ice like smoke, generated from two black boxes on either side of the pond. I blinked. Had those been there all day? She glided in a wide arc through the cloud, her thin lips stretched into a smile. This wasn't helping anything. It would discredit anything she said about the woods.

How could I stop her without making a bigger scene? I held my breath as her arms waved through the fog.

"She's pretty good," Cole said, hiding a smile behind his hand.

He was being generous. Ms. Krick's thin limbs were far from graceful, and if she'd ever had any training as a skater, she'd long forgotten it. Her movements jerked across the rough ice. She skipped along the far bank, swinging her arms in time to the music.

The laughter had turned to catcalls from the crowd.

"Who is this lady?" The guy next to us asked, looking bewildered.

I didn't recognize him from St. Augustus. I turned my back to the pond and spread my arms wide. Ava pushed her way to us.

"Did you know about this?" Ava's face was pale, reflected in the strong lights over the pond. She'd ditched the mask Jules had made her, and had thrown a black coat over the silver suit, its shiny leggings poking out below.

"No, it's awful," I said, giving her a complicit smile.

Ms. Krick's "performance" was like a train wreck I couldn't pull my eyes away from.

"She's ruining everything," Ava said, her voice beyond bitter. It hinted of fear.

"Ava, are you okay?" I asked.

Ava held her stomach and her eyes darted around like she was looking for a place to be sick. "Do you even want to stop the road?" she asked me.

"I do," I said, crossing my arms. I did. I didn't need to start over again. Maybe my horrible past had prepared me to appreciate how good things were now. I didn't need to erase it. "As much as you do."

Ava's hands shook.

"Ava, maybe we should get you out of the crowd." Was she having a panic attack? Cole was a short distance away, watching Ms. Krick skate with his eyes wide. Ava grabbed a fistful of my hoodie, pulling me to her.

"You don't understand." She shook her head wildly. "My Dad's wish. Without it I'd never have been born. If the fountain goes..." she trailed off.

"What?" Her words hit me like a sack of flour in the head. I stared at her.

"We have to stop her. She's making things worse," Ava said.

I nodded. If the fountain's wishes were reversed, Ava would die. Or disappear. Like I had, except, for good. My stomach twisted. "We can turn off the music. I think it's over by the stage,"

I said. Doing something, anything, was better than nothing. I guided Ava by the elbow.

"We'll be back," I called to Cole.

The music swelled to a crescendo and the smoke machine kept cranking out a sickly mess of white smog for Ms. Krick to twirl through. She did a heavy stag's leap across the ice. As she landed, a long CRACK resounded across the park. We froze as the crowd drew in a collective gasp. Ms. Krick, unaware of the danger she was suddenly in, waved and blew kisses as she spun in slow motion, only inches from a dark patch in the fog.

"She doesn't know the ice just cracked," Cole called to me.

He scrambled over the bank and onto the edge of the ice. Ava and I hurried after him, stumbling through the soft slush on the bank. "It's been warm all day. Nobody checked the ice." His eyes darted around the pond.

Ms. Krick smiled wide at the banks, where arms waved and yelled for her to turn around.

"Ms. Krick!" Ava called.

Ms. Krick waved back at her and continued skating, mistaking Ava's warning for praise.

"Behind you!" Ava tried again as we stopped a few feet into the pond. We couldn't go any further without risking the ice below us giving way.

Ms. Krick kept up her determined movements. The music sped up and she executed a sequence of ridiculous hops, ending in a twirl. As her feet thudded to the ice with the last hop, it gave way beneath her with a sickening boom that rippled through the park.

Shrieks from the bank drowned out my own thoughts.

"Cole!" I managed a garbled yell. He was several feet ahead of us, inching across the ice with careful steps. A hole the size of a large puddle had opened up under Ms. Krick's feet, swallowing her legs, then her shoulders and gray bun. Water bubbled up through the gap in the ice, flooding the surface, flowing over Cole's boots. Ms. Krick's drowning arms broke the surface, followed by her face, gray with panic. Her mouth gaped into an 'O', gasping like a guppy out of water. Her fingers scrabbled at the ragged edges of the hole she was in, desperate for traction. All around me, there were shouts and running. Only Cole was out past the edge of the ice. I was frozen to my spot.

"Cole needs us," Ava said. Her voice was too loud. She jiggled my elbow, tugging at me to go with her out onto the ice.

I gave my head a shake, focusing on Cole, who beckoned for us to follow.

"Stay low," he called, getting down on his belly.

Ethan and Jake skidded out onto the ice in their shoes, laying down behind Cole and grabbing each other's ankles. Jake was still dressed in his super hero king costume. His crown flew off his head and spun across the ice, landing in a puddle.

"They're forming a human chain." Ava's voice was foggy. "They need us."

Ms. Krick's face came up for air again, her arms flailing in the air and not grabbing onto anything before she submerged again.

"The boys will anchor us." Ava's voice was right in my ear. "I'll hold you and you grab for Ms. Krick. Stay as flat as you can."

"I can't." I jerked away from her grasp.

Ms. Krick surfaced for a third time, her eyes wild and trained on us. She didn't scream, but she didn't need to. Her eyes screamed.

"I- I'll be an anchor." My heart pounded. I wanted to help her but the ice was thin and there was so much water seeping across the ground. The task was hopeless.

Ava had her hands on her hips.

"The boys are stronger and we're lighter. It makes sense for them to hold us and for us to lay on the ice. We have a better chance at not falling through."

"Please," I said, as my voice cracked. "I'll hold your legs."

I couldn't even look at the watery hole, much less Ms. Krick's bobbing face. I turned away as she surfaced again with a splash.

"How do I know you won't drop me, if I do it?" Ava's eyes narrowed.

"Hurry!" Ethan yelled to us.

"I won't." I wouldn't but I could see why she thought I might. Ava gave me one last hard look then lay flat, slithering out on her belly toward the hole.

"Courtney, grab on to her!" Cole yelled.

I snapped out of whatever trance I'd been in, easing myself down as quickly as I dared. I combat-crawled my way across the waterlogged ice. Freezing water seeped up my sleeves and my hair hung loose around my jawline, freezing to the ice every time I stopped for a moment then yanking free, breaking off strands as I inched forward in slow motion.

Cole's grip was like iron shackles snapped around my ankles. I reached for Ava's legs above her boots and squeezed tight until my knuckles ached. The material of her silver leggings was thin and I could feel her warmth. She looked back once over her shoulder and our gazed locked. I wouldn't let go. I gave her a small nod and she stretched for Ms. Krick, who I couldn't see from my vantage point. The shouting around us died down and all I could hear was the slapping of water against the ice underneath me and Ms. Krick's gasps, although I might have imagined that.

"Don't let go!" Ava called as she strained forward.

I didn't answer, but tightened my grip even further to reassure her. My hands had gone numb where they touched the ice.

"Ooohh." A gurgled cry from up ahead sent a ripple through my core. I lifted my head over Ava's boots to see Ms. Krick's hand slip from Ava's grasp and disappear under the water. I sucked in a breath.

"I can't get her!" Ava's frustrated cry rang out across the ice. My grip was so tight I could feel her legs shiver. "I'm going to dive under! Everyone ready?"

"Ready!" yelled Cole from behind.

"We've got you anchored from the shore with the whole team!" called Jake. "Do what you need to."

I pressed my stomach into the ice, bracing for the strain that came moments later with a jerk. I yelled out with gut-wrenching effort as Ava's ankles slid past my palms and I dug my fingernails into the cuff of her leather boots. I still had her, or at least I had her feet. The rest of her body plunged under the surface of the water. A shuddering crack in the ice split under Ava and spread until it slithered under my chin, then under my belly. More water bubbled up under my hoodie, but the ice surface below me stayed solid. I held my breath. My arms shook with effort.

A force tugged at my hands, lurching me forward. Our human chain sagged like a fishing line weighted at the end with its catch.

"Have you got her?" Cole yelled to Ava from behind me.

Ava didn't answer. My elbows ached, about to pop off, leaving the rest of my arm behind.

"She does," I called, through clenched teeth. "Pull!" I gave the command that Ava couldn't. Her head was still underwater.

My feet yanked backward. I curled my toes and flexed my feet to keep my boots from sliding clean off in Cole's hands. My hoodie rode up on my torso, exposing my bare midriff, which scraped against the rough ice, burning my skin. I dug my nails into the seam above the soles of Ava's boots, barely holding on. But I still didn't let go. My eyes rolled back in my head as my vision clouded. I channeled all my energy into my hands where they were connected to Ava.

My feet lifted as I was dragged off the ice and dusty snow filled my boots. We'd reached the bank. A cheer went up all around me. I held on. There were two more links in our chain that needed to be safe before I could relax.

"She's not breathing," Ava yelled, gasping as she hit the snow in front of me. She scrambled to her feet, shaking her boots free of my grasp. I lay on the bank, panting, tears stinging my eyes.

"Courtney, are you okay?" Cole kneeled beside me with his hands gently squeezing my shoulders.

"I'm fine," I whispered. A shiver rocked through me as reality came into focus. I took Cole's hand and tugged on it, hoisting myself up. This wasn't over yet. Ms. Krick needed help and everyone was standing around, in shock. There was work to be done.

"Can you manage CPR?" Ava sputtered. Her teeth chattered. She didn't need to ask if I knew how. We spent our days in the pool. I'd done a refresher CPR course just before Christmas. The steps were emblazoned on my mind.

"I've got her," I confirmed. "Get her warm," I called to the others. I was soaked and cold myself, but Ava was spent from her time under the icy water.

Jackets appeared from the crowd, passed from hand to hand.

"You did great." I gave Ava a weak smile of apology. She'd been brave when fear had stopped me. The thin ice had thrown me, I hadn't known what to do.

Ms. Krick had been under the water. She'd been drowning.

I hadn't seen a person stop breathing first hand, either, but I'd trained for it. I'd leaned CPR. I could do this. I turned to see to Ms. Krick, who lay shriveled and lifeless on the bank.

CHAPTER SEVENTEEN

Ava

Ethan heaped a thick down coat over me and scooped me up, running with me cradled in his arms across the park. My wet hair was plastered against his chest and the urge to sleep overcame me. My eyelids fluttered closed and the rhythmic motion of his stride lulled me under. Courtney had taken over CPR. She would know what to do, I saw it in her eyes. I could rest.

I was vaguely aware of passing through a gate, which Ethan kicked open with a clatter. My body trembled and there was something I was probably supposed to do to stay warm. My eyelids were made of lead and wouldn't stay open.

Ethan shouted up at a house and then we were inside, where I was laid on soft cushions.

"Can we get some blankets?" Ethan asked, his voice sharp.

I rolled inward on the couch, which smelled of baby powder. Where had all these people come from? The ends of my fingertips ached with cold. My soaked outfit clung to me and the blankets around me smelled of damp.

"Ava, drink this." Ethan rolled me by the shoulder onto my back. He crouched on the floor beside me, holding something warm to my lips. "Cole's mom made you tea."

I blinked as my surroundings came into focus. The musty room was familiar. We were in Cole's living room. Ethan propped up my head with a pillow and held the warm mug to my lips. Its steam filled my nostrils, but it was too hot to drink. I gave a small shake of my head and he pulled it away.

"Thank you," was all I could manage, my limbs were so weak. "Is Ms. Krick okay?"

"Courtney and Cole stayed with her," he said. "You did everything you could. You were amazing." His lips pulled into a thin smile, which didn't reassure me.

Ms. Krick's lips had been blue. I'd left her with Courtney, who should have the same emergency training I had, if she'd completed her swim levels, although I didn't know that for sure. Maybe I should have stayed. Mustering my energy, I pushed myself up on my elbows. Ms. Krick wasn't my favorite teacher. Arguably, she made the bottom of my list. But she was full of life. She didn't care that the crowd laughed at her efforts, which had been to save the woods.

"If Ms. Krick dies..." I trailed off, pushing myself to a sitting position. My voice was slurred. If Ms. Krick died, we'd be on our own to fight for the woods. And we might never know what she was really after. That hit me hard, like a punch in the gut.

"Shh." Ethan pushed my damp hair from my forehead, easing me back down on the pillow. He leaned in close, rubbing my arms through the layers of blankets. My shivering lessened. Sirens blared outside. "The paramedics are here. You're going to be fine."

"Let go of me!" A shrieking voice came from the back door, tearing through my aching head. My hands flew to cover my ears. Her voice scratched like fingernails down the inside of my skull, even as a warmth spread inside me to hear it.

"Ma'am, you need to let us help you," a woman's deep voice spoke with authority.

Ms. Krick was alive and kicking. I covered my eyes with my arm. I could rest.

"I'm going to guess she's fine," Ethan said, nudging me.

I peeked out from under my arm. A woman in a navy uniform with a yellow paramedic crest on the sleeve restrained a feisty Ms. Krick by wrapping a shimmering silver emergency blanket around her shoulders.

"I haven't even made my speech yet!" Ms. Krick insisted,

beating the paramedic's chest with her undersized fists. Her efforts bounced off the woman's uniform like rain off a roof. "They don't know! They don't know *why*."

My ears perked up.

"She's over here," another woman's voice came from the hall. Two paramedics jogged through the archway toward me. I craned my neck to see Ms. Krick, but two men blocked my view, one tall with brown skin, one short and pale, with wispy blond hair thinning across his forehead.

"I've been keeping her warm," Ethan told them. "She didn't want the tea."

The short blond man's gloved hands swiped something over my forehead then pressed two fingers against my neck. "Her pulse could be stronger," he said, over his shoulder to the tall paramedic, who wasted no time producing tubing from the zippered kit he brought.

The tall man frowned with serious concentration. "Can you take your shirt off?" he asked.

I balked. What?

"You'll warm up faster without the wet layers next to you," he said.

"I'll be over here," Ethan said quickly, moving away from the couch and sitting with his back turned to me on a large overstuffed ottoman in the middle of the room.

But that was the least of my worries. The smaller paramedic deftly helped me wiggle out of the thin synthetic shirt Jules had fashioned for me, draping a paper gown over me. Under a blanket, I then peeled off the soaked silver leggings, which sucked against my wet skin. I dropped the discarded outfit on the carpet next to the couch, its stretchy fabric forming a very small pile.

Mr. Tall connected tubes to a metal stand, with a pole he unfolded and snapped into place. My field of vision was expanding.

"You call yourself a medical professional?"

Five or six more paramedics were bent over a complaining Ms. Krick across the room. "And your best advice is to take off my clothes?" she said. "I will not!"

A snort escaped through my nostrils. She really *was* fine. Mr. Tall held my hand, flipping my palm down. "Don't move," he said.

I flinched as the needle stabbed into the back of my hand.

"Would you like some more tea?" Cole's mom, Brenda, wasn't dressed for work that night. She was wearing trim yoga pants and a matching sweatshirt, zipped up the front.

"No, thanks," I said. My mouth was dry, but I didn't have the energy to drink anything. I hadn't touched the tea she'd already sent. It must be around somewhere.

"Thanks, Mrs. Coffman," Ethan said, his manners were impeccable, as ever. He crouched by the couch again, kissing my forehead.

Mrs. Coffman flitted off to the other side of the room, where Ms. Krick was being attended to.

"You!" Ms. Krick's voice shrilled right through my temples, stabbing a needle into the middle of my brain as I cringed. "You call yourself a mayor! I spit on your actions."

"The mayor is here?" I craned my neck to see, the weight of the new blankets the paramedics heaped on me holding me back.

Ethan shrugged, but followed my gaze.

"I don't want to spend another moment in this house. The house your daddy stole from my family," Ms. Krick said. Two paramedics held her arms. She had an IV pole attached to her and a tube fitted into her nose, but that didn't stop her from jumping up and down, shaking her fists at Cole's mom.

My eyes widened. "Cole's *mom* is the mayor?"

Ethan scrambled to his feet, hurrying across the room.

The short paramedic's hands were on my shoulders, stopping me from jumping up.

"You need to rest," Mr. Short said. "And you're connected to the pole. So just try to sleep. Everything over there's under control."

"Where is it?" Ms. Krick demanded, charging at Cole's mom, tugging against the apologetic paramedics. "Where's the other stone?"

Ethan spun to face me, catching my eye. He'd been right. The stone in the dining room had something to do with Ms. Krick and possibly Izzy.

"It is my birthright. I am the great granddaughter of Isaac Young and what's his is mine. The woods are mine!"

I would have laughed if anything about Ms. Krick's wild eyes were funny. She was still wearing her skating costume, its collar torn to ribbons and the bodice streaked with dirt. Thankfully, her skates had been removed. Her stockinged feet barely touched the ground as she tried to gain traction against the arms holding her back.

"I don't know what you're talking about." Cole's mom backed away from the scene, with her hands in front of her like she was ready to push if Ms. Krick burst out of her restraints.

"Sedate her," the first paramedic woman barked. Her face was crimson with the effort of keeping Ms. Krick's flailing hands from hitting her.

"Now, Matilda," said Cole's dad as he strode in, brushing shoulders with Ethan, who slipped from the room, giving me a pointed look. Mr. Coffman ran a hand through his sparse brown hair.

"You've had a nasty accident here. I understand you're upset about the road but times change. We have to change with them. The school's agreed."

Cole had said his dad supported the road. Mr. Coffman worked in the city planning office but Mrs. Coffman was the mayor of Evergreen.

"It's my birthright!" Ms. Krick hopped from one foot to the other. Her blue hospital gown gaped open at her neck, where folds of her skin hung like a necklace. Her collarbone stuck out against her paper-thin skin. Her face was animated, her eyebrows wagging up and down. She gave off so much energy that it was hard to tell that she'd just almost drowned, except that her hair was dark and wet, sticking out from her head.

I wrapped my bottom blanket around my torso, letting the others fall as I sat up. "I'm fine," I said to Mr. Short. I'd only been under the water for a moment. Ms. Krick's skating costume had shredded in my hands as I pulled at it, the water sucking her under. Just before the last jerking pull came, I wove my fingers into her hair, pulling her out by her bun.

Headmistress Valentine swept into the room. "Matilda, stop this nonsense, right now," she said.

I sat bolt upright. Valentine's hair was askew, her face purple with rage.

"I should have listened to the board. This fiasco of a carnival never should have been allowed. Your time at St. Augustus has run its course," the headmistress loomed over Ms. Krick.

Ethan reappeared, standing frozen in the archway to the living room. We exchanged a look. Our headmistress was dressing Krick down in front of everyone. She was firing our English teacher, who had been at the school so long she'd taught our parents.

While my heart lifted to think my English marks might go up without Ms. Krick's critical eye on my papers, stopping the road without her would be a steeper battle.

"She needs to rest," the lady paramedic said, unfolding another blanket and wrapping it around an indignant Ms. Krick's shoulders.

Ms. Krick was being *fired* for fighting the road. For protecting the fountain.

Mr. Coffman stood to the side with his arms crossed. He wore a smug smile.

"Yes, Matilda," Headmistress Valentine said. "A rest is just what you need. The board is insisting on your retirement. Immediately."

Mr. Coffman's smile widened. He cleared his throat, covering his mouth with his fist. My trembles had started again. I shouldn't be here, witnessing this moment.

Ms. Krick shook her feeble fist at nobody in particular. "On my agreed terms?"

Headmistress Valentine nodded. "Yes, yes. It will all happen tomorrow."

Tomorrow. Tomorrow was Sunday. My jaw dropped. Ms. Krick was being forced to retire. Was that even legal? And why was she smiling?

Ms. Krick's gaze lighted on Mr. Coffman. "What are you

staring at? What have you done to protect the legacy of the school? I have dedicated my life. And you... you!" She rushed at him, but stopped short as the paramedics caught her by the arms.

"Matilda!" Headmistress Valentine stepped between Krick and her intended target.

Ethan stepped to Mr. Coffman's side. "Mr. Coffman, perhaps it would be better if you moved to the hall?" he said, taking Cole's dad by the shoulders.

I strained against the tubes connecting me to the IV pole, leaning forward in my seat. There was nothing I could do. Mr. Coffman shrugged Ethan off.

"She's nuts." Mr. Coffman shook his head as he backed away from Ethan. "Magic, or no."

Ethan's head snapped up at the mention of magic. Ethan looked my way and I nodded. He'd said *magic*.

Ms. Krick pointed at Cole's Dad. "This man stole from my family."

What was she accusing him of?

"Do something," Headmistress Valentine pleaded with the paramedics, as she held Ms. Krick upright.

The woman standing nearest sprang into action, guiding Krick back to the couch and holding her fingers to Krick's neck. "Her heart rate is through the roof. We'll have to sedate her."

Ms. Krick's face was turning purple. Headmistress Valentine nodded. "That seems best," she agreed.

"Arrest him!" Ms. Krick screeched. Her laser focus was trained on Mr. Coffman. She was completely unaware of the conversation happening around her, deciding her fate. Her eyes flashed with revenge.

The woman who'd brought her had a needle in her hand. She stretched around Ms. Krick and jammed it into her rear.

"Aargh!" Ms. Krick's garbled scream jolted through me as she slumped against the couch cushions, guided by the two attendants beside her. She lay lifeless, just as she'd looked on bank of the pond.

My mouth gaped open. If my pulse was weak before, it thrummed now.

"Ava!" Dad came crashing into the chaos, through the archway that led to the front door. His glasses were crooked and his jacket looked like he slept in it. "I came as soon as I heard. I'm so sorry I wasn't there, I..." He wiped a tear roughly with his sleeve, adjusting his thick black rimmed glasses.

"Dad, I'm okay." I hugged him back as best I could without pulling the IV line out of my hand.

"Is she hypothermic?" Dad asked the paramedic.

"She was, mildly, after being in the water. Her vitals are all stable now. She should take it easy, but she'll make a full recovery."

"Oh, hey Mr. Marshall." Ethan held out a bundle of clothes to me. "Cole got you some clothes." He tossed the sweat pants and hoodie at me, covering my head.

"Thanks," I mumbled. The activity had awakened my senses. I was even starting to get warm.

"And thank you for taking such good care of my daredevil daughter," Dad said to Mr. Short. "Can I take her back to the school?"

"She's very brave," Mr. Short answered. "And she knew what to do. Most people don't know to stay low on the ice."

"Cole acted fast," I said. I'd seen that kind of rescue on TV, but it wasn't something we learned, even swimming as much as I did, in California. Cole had taken charge. He'd made the rescue possible. Where was Cole? And Courtney? Ethan said Cole had gotten me these clothes.

"Her vitals are stable, she's going to be fine," Mr. Short told Dad. "She should get plenty of rest."

"Well, it's not exactly restful here," I pointed out, gesturing to the scene we'd just witnessed on the other side of the living room.

"She'll rest," Dad chimed in.

Mr. Short nodded. "I'll take her IV out," he said. "Are you feeling better?"

I nodded emphatically. The commotion was over. It was time to go. I wanted to go. We had more to do.

Mr. Short removed the needle from the back of my hand,

pressing some gauze and a bandage over the trace of blood that remained.

"Here, let me help you." Dad jumped in, threading Cole's Evergreen High hoodie over my head. Ethan grabbed another blanket, holding its green wool up as a screen against the rest of the room, which had quieted.

I tugged the black sweats over my calves, wriggling into them with as much modesty as I could muster. The waist bagged around mine. I rolled the band over twice to form a makeshift belt.

"I can take her back to school," Ethan offered.

"I'll drive you both," Dad said. "You really saved Ms. Krick?" He looked over his shoulder at Ms. Krick, who slept peacefully on the couch, covered with a blanket. Valentine and the Coffmans had gone.

"I guess so," I mumbled.

It was weird to have Dad there. I missed him, but I was still getting to know this Dad. The one who wanted to be involved with everything about St. Augustus. The one I'd created, with my wish.

Dad chuckled. "I might have let her sink, just a little," he said.

I swatted his arm. "Dad!"

"Not really," he admitted. "Still, you risked a lot going out onto the ice. I'll be having a word with the school about making sure you kids are safe."

I shrugged. "Swimming is what I do. I would have been fine."

"I guess it ended well," he said.

Cole's living room was a wreck, with medical supplies covering the patterned carpet and more paramedics traipsing through with their boots. The three of us picked our way past the commotion and I hung back as Dad and Ethan spilled out into the hall. Headmistress Valentine stood in the archway, watching the peaceful Ms. Krick.

"Headmistress?" I said.

She shook her head like she was coming back from a far away day dream. "Ava, how are you feeling?"

"I'm fine," I assured her. "What were Ms. Krick's demands, for her retirement?"

"Oh, it's a lark," she said, tossing off its importance. "She wants to be an honorary student for a day."

I frowned. Of all the sentimental things. It had nothing to do with the road.

"Get some sleep," she said, smiling kindly. "You were very brave today."

"Thanks," I said. I'd expected something more of Ms. Krick's request. Something craftier.

"Ready?" Dad asked, pulling on his boots.

"I don't have any shoes." I looked down at my bare feet. I had no idea where my boots had gone.

"I'll piggyback you," Ethan offered, turning his back to me and holding out his arms.

"Ava!" Courtney emerged from the dining room. She was also clad in an outfit of ill-fitting sweats, with a football team logo on them. "We were so worried. How are you feeling?"

"Courtney," I said. I stopped beside a table in the hall, leaning on it. She could have let go of my feet and let me drown with Ms. Krick, but she didn't. I'd curled my frozen toes to keep my boots from sliding off my feet and she'd held on. It couldn't have been easy. "Thank you. For holding onto me."

Her brow furrowed. "Of course."

"I mean, I know how hard it was to hang on. I nearly couldn't get Ms. Krick. Thank you."

Her face relaxed into a smile.

"Ava! I found your boots." Cole joined us in the hall. "They've been on the radiator. They're warm, but not that dry."

"Thanks." I took them from Cole and winced as I slipped my bare feet into their warm, damp liners.

"Ava tells me you were the one who knew what to do on the ice." Dad put out his hand to shake Cole's. "Thank you."

"Thanks, Mr. Marshall," Cole said. "I grew up with the pond in our backyard. It was drilled into us what to do if the ice ever gave out. I've never had occasion to try it though. That was a first."

"You didn't tell us your mom was the mayor," I said.

Cole nodded. I saw a look pass between him and Courtney.

Her mouth pursed.

"I spent the day trying to get the school buildings recognized as historical landmarks," Dad said. "But even if I could figure out the paperwork to protect the buildings, it wouldn't help the woods."

So, that's where he'd been all day.

"I noticed the plaque outside," he said to Cole, nodding to the front door. "Your house is protected. I'd love to talk with your dad about the process."

Cole laughed. "Dad's hiding upstairs. Ms. Krick's outburst left him a little spent. He's the one who signed the deal for the road." He cast a sideways look at Courtney, who eyed him. Her arms were crossed.

Dad frowned. "The deal's a bad one for the school."

"I know. That's why I was helping fight it," Cole said. "It looked hopeless, I'll admit. But the idea of historical protection is an interesting angle."

Courtney still hadn't said anything, her face pale.

"What about the house on the other side of the woods?" Cole asked. "Could it be recognized?"

Dad shook his head. "That's my mother-in-law's house. It isn't old enough for protection and hasn't got an interesting enough history. Besides, it was renovated pretty heavily in the late sixties when they bought it. Most of the inside reflects that era."

"Gran is happy about selling to the city," I said.

"She told me," Dad confirmed, his mouth pulled into a line. "There used to be ruins at the south end of the woods. Are they still there?"

"I've seen them," Courtney stepped forward. "The site was Isaac Young's home as a child. It's why he built the school on the land."

All of our heads whipped toward her. Courtney's eyes brightened. "I can show you."

Dad gave a low whistle. "That could be enough. Lead the way, Courtney. Let's go see what's left of the house." He paused. The screen door slammed behind me as I joined them on the porch. "Oh, Ava. You probably need to change and get warm."

"No, I'm fine."

If Courtney was leading Dad to Isaac Young's childhood home, I was going. The circulation and feeling had returned to my feet. Ethan put a jacket around my shoulders and I wrapped it around me. "We can go back to the school, if you want," he said.

Dad's van was parked on Cole's street behind a line of ambulances and we trudged along the sidewalk to it. Courtney and Cole's heads were bent low together in front of us.

"I'm feeling better." I plastered on a smile brighter than I felt. I really just wanted to sleep. But I wasn't ready to be alone and Ethan couldn't come into the dorm. Besides, this was the biggest break we'd had to protect the woods and we were running out of time.

Dad opened the sliding door to the van and we paused awkwardly, none of us getting in.

"Ava, you should take the front seat," Courtney said.

"I'd rather sit with Ethan," I replied, leaning in to his body under the arm he had around me. His warmth was the only thing keeping me standing. Courtney shrugged and took the front seat without a look back at Cole. Her chill rocked through me.

I settled into the bench seat at the back, my toes and fingers still tingling from their earlier trauma.

"Ava, you don't look so good," Ethan whispered, as he squeezed my arm.

"Thanks?" I said, grimacing. I was a little dizzy, but this was important. Dad wouldn't let me come if it wasn't. "I'm fine."

"This is it?" Dad kicked at the low remains of a wall that Courtney said was part of Isaac Young's childhood home. The stone glowed in the moonlight. "I remembered there being more."

"Maybe it's deteriorated since you were last here?" Cole said.

"Maybe." Dad pulled his weight up onto the wall, standing on top with his hands on his hips. "More likely, it was always like this. My memory sometimes plays tricks on me. Mariam knew every inch of these woods."

I winced as he said Mom's name. We'd lived together so many years where it hadn't crossed his lips. I wasn't used to it slipping out so easily. Mom had shown me the clearing where the fountain was. She must have shown Dad, too.

Ethan clambered up to stand on the wall beside Dad, while my feet stayed planted on the ground. Their silhouettes were black against the night sky. Ethan was as tall as Dad. My boots were no longer wet, but the warmth from Cole's radiator had long fled. "What do you think, Cole?" Ethan asked.

"These ruins aren't enough." Cole picked at the moss-eaten stones piled where a doorway once stood. "The historical designation is meant to preserve architectural examples of different periods. This won't qualify."

Where was Courtney? She'd wandered away, standing in a field fifty yards from what was left of Isaac Young's house. Long grass poked through a crust of snow on the ground, brushing her knees. She had on a wool beanie and thick gloves that would be welcome on my frozen ears and hands.

"Did you find something?" Ethan called to her.

I huddled at the end of the property, wringing my cold hands together. This place was a dead end and I wasn't dressed to be out here.

Courtney kicked at the ground, making a pile of sodden snow with her boot. She had her phone out with her flashlight pointed at the ground. "Will a grave do?" she called back.

What did she mean, a *grave*? Dad and Ethan jumped down off the wall and Cole strode into the field. Courtney's mouth twisted into a sideways smile, as though she remembered something funny.

"Whoa," Cole said. Both his and Courtney's gazes were trained on the grass as I shuffled over to join them, my hands balled into fists in the sleeves of Ethan's coat.

"Who's Alexandrina Young?" Ethan asked, reading the name chiseled on the flat stone as I peered over his shoulder.

"She was Isaac Young's mother," Courtney replied. "And Isaac's and his father James' graves are over here." She pointed and kneeled down to dig in the snow with her mittens. Cole dropped to his knees beside her, clearing away snow with the sleeve of his jacket.

My shiver this time wasn't from the cold. I'd only been to

Mom's grave the day she was buried, and not since. Isaac Young's body was just ten yards away from me, or his bones anyway, frozen under the ground. I didn't need to get any closer.

Dad, on the other hand, cheered out loud. "Yes!" he exclaimed, kneeling down beside them, kissing the snow-covered grass. "We can work with this. Isaac's body just might stop the road."

Ethan beamed beside Dad and Cole laughed. Dad's hand clap echoed off the nearby woods. I smacked my lips against the cold. My mouth tasted sour. How could people be buried out here?

"We can save the fountain," Courtney agreed.

"The what?" Cole looked perplexed, as the rest of us stared. He didn't know what we were fighting for. Courtney's face blanched. She hadn't told him. My heart went out to her.

The wind moaned through the treetops.

"I can show you," she said, finally, lowering her eyes and turning her collar up against the wind.

My eyes narrowed. Cole wouldn't be able to see the fountain. He wasn't a student at St. Augustus.

"There's something you all need to see." Her voice dipped.

"What?" Cole looked to the rest of us for help, but Ethan just shrugged, staying silent.

"It's this way," Courtney said, waving us toward the woods. Her hair whipped like fire around her shoulders as she strode ahead and disappeared into the trees.

There was nothing for us to do but follow.

CHAPTER EIGHTEEN

Ava

Ethan caught up to me and took my bare hand in his glove as we picked our way between the trees. I held a branch back for Dad to get through behind us with my free hand. There was no path in this unused part of the woods. Dad grabbed the branch from me. Heat rushed to my cheeks as he grinned down at my other hand, clasped in Ethan's.

"Where are we going?" Cole asked Courtney.

The treetops overhead blocked out the starlight. The woods were full of shadows. A squirrel scurried overhead.

"I-I can't really explain," she replied. "You'll have to see for yourself."

"Will Cole be able to see anything?" Ethan asked. "I think I'm the only one here that can still see the fountain."

"I don't know," Courtney said. "But we're not going to the fountain."

What was she playing at?

"Why couldn't I see it?" Cole asked. "How can Ethan see something and I can't?"

Dad gave a nervous chuckle. Ethan and I exchanged a look. If Cole couldn't see whatever Courtney was going to show us, he'd think we were nuts.

"I think it's this way." Courtney hesitated at a concentration of tree trunks where we had to choose whether to go around it to the left or right. We followed her blindly. She hadn't let go of my feet when we lay on the thin ice of the pond. I hadn't drowned. Maybe she'd changed.

Courtney slowed at a grove of bushy evergreens. We'd reached the edge of the clearing, where its long grass poked up through the snow. As expected, there was no fountain.

"She's taking us to the wall," Ethan said, under his breath.

"Isn't this where you rescued Husk, the day we met?" Cole's freckles wrinkled with his nose.

Courtney nodded.

"The trees are so overgrown." Dad gave a low whistle, his eyes darting nervously around the clearing.

"It'll be a tight fit, but we have to climb under to see it," Courtney said.

"Under the trees?" Dad asked, frowning.

"Mom didn't show you the wall of wishes?" I asked. Maybe mom had never found it. Dad shook his head.

"So, maybe we *can* teach you a thing or two about your school?" Ethan teased.

"Have you touched it?" Courtney asked me, wheeling around, a hint of excitement in her voice.

"I think so?" I said. We'd definitely touched it, although nothing had happened.

"You'd know if you had," she said.

"We wiped the snow off it with our gloves," Ethan said.

"You've both been here?" Courtney asked, looking between Ethan and me.

"Yes," I said, crossing my arms.

She'd dragged us here for nothing.

"If you were wearing gloves, maybe it didn't work," she said.

"Courtney, why don't you just show us what you found?" Dad said, lifting a branch and peering underneath.

Courtney nodded, ducking under the branch Dad held. "Squeeze in behind me everyone," she said.

Ethan and I still held hands. Together, we ducked in after her, followed by Dad and finally, Cole. The space under the trees had been close when Ethan and I had been here before, the site of the kiss that had made everything clear. The moment I'd known that I wanted to be with him through whatever came our way. And there had been a lot. The tight den smelled of pine needles and peat. We crawled in on all fours. My knees scraped against the icy ground, bringing flashback of my earlier near-drowning while crawling across the ice. Pine needles grabbed at my hair.

Cole gave a nervous laugh "This is spooky," he said. "I'm sure you have a good reason for packing us in here like sardines, Courtney?"

I rocked back to a sitting position, jammed between Dad and Ethan. My back pressed against a tree trunk. Our body warmth hung humidly in the air.

Courtney pulled the previously broken branches off the wall of wishes and fired up the flashlight on her phone. I hugged my knees to my chest. Despite the chill from the ground, being squished between Dad and Ethan was the warmest I'd been since I'd left the safety of Cole's couch.

"Is it a wall?" Cole leaned in.

"It's the wall of wishes," Courtney said.

I stifled a yawn. Courtney could have shown Cole this without dragging the rest of us along.

"Ava, come put your hand on the wall." Courtney's eyes shone in the dim light.

"I've seen the wall," I said, comfortable in my cocoon. "Let Dad see it."

"You haven't touched it." Her voice was low. The space was closing in on me. Were there new wishes? Is that what she wanted to show us? A wave of curiosity got the better of me and I crawled between Ethan and Cole to get to the wall. "Touch it," she said.

When Ethan and I had discovered the wall before Christmas, letters glowed at the bottom of the list. Ethan's wish, the one he never actually made. *I wish for Ava.* The fountain had known his heart. It had been ready to grant it. But Ethan hadn't made that wish. He hadn't needed to. A rush prickled up the nape of my neck. Was his almost-wish still there? Had he come back and thrown a coin?

I squinted at the wall, where Courtney's phone shone. My wish was still the last one there. My shoulders relaxed. Of course, he wouldn't wish for me. He didn't need to. He'd won me over fair and square. I gave him a sheepish smile.

"Are those *wishes* from the fountain?" Dad asked. His breath was close in my ear. His eyes bulged at the wall, over my shoulder.

"All of them," Courtney confirmed.

"I wish St. Augustus had never heard of Courtney or her family." My stomach tightened as Dad read my wish out loud. I wished I could erase it from the stone but there were no more wishes to be had. That was the only one I was given.

"Is this wall part of the grave site?" Cole asked, frowning.

He had no idea what we were about to tell him.

I stretched my hand to the wall, running my bare fingertips over the stone where Ethan's wish had been sketched. Sketched, but not finalized. It was just stone. My fingertips brushed the top of the gray wall. Cold seeped into my hand as I pressed my palm against the rock.

"Can you see it?" Courtney's voice was pitchy.

"See what?" I turned my head without breaking contact with the wall. And then Courtney's face blurred in front of my eyes, replaced with vivid color. I jerked my hand back.

"Did you see it?" Courtney asked again.

My eyes widened. The image faded and the den was dark again, with only Courtney's phone lighting the wall. I extended my hand again. There had been light. And movement. My vision clouded again as I lay my palms on the cold stone. The stone held the magic of everyone's wishes that had ever been made on the fountain.

A cloud of light surrounded me. Everyone around me faded into the background, although Ethan and Dad still pressed on my sides. Like a movie playing around me, scenes came to life, filling me with memories flooding from the wall.

"Oh..." My mouth opened and closed.

"What is it?" Dad's voice was in my ear. I shrugged his hand off my shoulder. I didn't want to break my connection.

"Go ahead, touch the wall," Courtney urged him.

One by one, Dad, Ethan, and Cole placed their hands against the stone. In a moment, memories of students past swirled around us all, sucking us into their vibrance, their light.

Ethan let out a low whistle. "Unbelievable."

"Mariam!" Dad cried out.

Holograms of Mom and Dad danced around us. It was their senior prom, with Mom's beautiful electric blue dress, the one she'd written about in her diary, floating around her. She'd bought that dress because it was David Roth's favorite color. She'd planned to go to prom with him. But Dad's wish had changed her mind and the rest, including their marriage and me being born, became history.

"What's happening? What are we seeing?" Cole asked. His voice was full of wonder. The four of us kneeled shoulder to shoulder as if we were praying at an altar instead of at a snow-covered wall under the trees.

"It's wishes," I whispered. I didn't want to interrupt the details I witnessed by speaking too loudly and interfering with the magic. I soaked it in. Student after student glided before us, throwing their coins, speaking their wishes at the fountain. My every sense flooded with alternate timelines. Dizzying. Interactions that had been erased, mixed with those who'd gone before. It was like a movie, except with feelings, senses, and imagery larger than life.

"It's all the wishes the fountain has ever granted." My eyes adjusted to a past Courtney floating before us, her face flushed with red cheeks. Her battle against the urge to fulfill her wish rattled through my bones. This bewitched Courtney's eyes squeezed shut, her hands in fists in the clearing. My hand was still on the wall, but my mind filled with pasts that could have been. Futures that might never be.

"What are we seeing?" asked Cole.

He was seeing it too, even though he wasn't a student. Isaac Young's journals said only students could see the fountain but this wall was permanent. It didn't disappear after we made the wishes. They were recorded forever and were here for anyone who stumbled under the stand of trees. Unless it was flattened to build a road.

The flood of images played on a loop. I'd seen this part, where my wish rippled through my family, our past. I saw too when Courtney threw a coin into the empty clearing, wishing she'd never heard of St. Augustus, just as she'd said. The wish I'd made for her. Granted by the fountain. Or me. Or some combination of the two.

The scenes painted themselves on my brain as if my hands were connected to a USB that downloaded into me. An electric jolt ripped up my arm as I broke the connection with the wall. I gasped. The images playing around me faded like smoke blown away by the wind, their colors lagging behind like waves dragging across sand.

I'd almost forgotten where we were, crouched under the trees. Everything was dusky around me as my eyes adjusted to the dim light. Courtney's flashlight had gone out. My knees ached from supporting my own weight. Ethan, Cole and Dad's mouths hung open. Their eyes glazed. Their hands were still on the wall. Courtney sat with her back pressed against a tree, watching us, watching me.

"Did these things happen?" Cole asked, to nobody in particular. He'd broken his connection to the wall and sat dazed, his shoulders slumped. He and Courtney had been on the highlight reel. They'd dated before my wish. It hadn't worked out. I winced. He was learning all this for the first time. I hoped for Courtney's sake he could handle it.

Courtney's stare calmed my mind enough to think. Silence settled like a blanket over all of us, as Dad broke his connection by moving his hands from the wall then Ethan did the same.

"Ms. Krick," I said. Even as I worked through the implications of what I was about to say, my heart rate skyrocketed. "I know why she wants to be a student. We have to stop her."

CHAPTER NINETEEN

Ava

"Does everyone at St. Augustus know about the fountain?" Cole was breathless. The five of us hurried across the school lawn, with me leading the way.

"Valentine doesn't," Ethan replied. "We can't just go to her."

"What choice do we have?" I asked, without breaking stride. Ice crunched under my boots as we neared the main building. It loomed ahead and visions of storming a castle came to mind. We had to tell the queen that a wicked witch was plotting. But plotting what exactly? My legs were weary but I couldn't stop. If Ms. Krick became a student for a day, she would find the fountain. Dread stirred in the pit of my stomach.

"The two of you watched Krick get fired and you didn't think to tell us?" Dad said, breathless.

I shrugged. "Valentine called it retirement. Ms. Krick will be named student for a day tomorrow, Valentine agreed to it. Ms. Krick will be able to see the fountain." My legs weren't as sure as usual as we ran, but adrenaline coursed through them, propelling me.

"She's had decades to think of her wish," Dad said, voicing my thoughts. "And she may have finally found a loophole. I can't even guess what she's planning. The fountain is powerful. We can't take the chance."

"I'll understand if you don't want to come," Courtney said to

Cole in a low voice where they jogged behind us. "I'm sorry I didn't tell you about the fountain. It's been eating me up inside."

I didn't want to listen to their conversation, but they were only a few feet behind us. I could almost hear Courtney's insides crumple as he didn't answer her right away. A quick glance over my shoulder confirmed that they'd stopped walking. Ethan, Dad, and I pressed on, leaving them on the lawn. I didn't envy Courtney. I'd been there.

"So, Mr. Marshall, what's the plan?" Ethan asked, as I tugged on the oversized black doors.

"Our story is crazy enough it might just work," Dad said. "They've agreed to make her a student for the day tomorrow. Headmistress Valentine has been here for years. She must have heard rumors of the fountain."

We rounded the stone hallway that led to the office.

"It doesn't matter if Valentine believes in the fountain," I said. "We just need her to see that Ms. Krick had a sneaky reason for demanding to be a student. She'll have to put the brakes on it." That is, if there was even anyone at the office. It was late on Saturday night, almost eleven o'clock.

I held out hope because Valentine had just fired a teacher and agreed to honor her in the morning. There had to be paperwork or something to take care of, despite the hour. Light spilled out from under the main office door and my heart lifted.

"I guess we'll find out?" Ethan said.

The door wasn't locked. The musty smell of the office threw me right back to my first day at St. Augustus, when Courtney had locked my clothes in my locker at the pool. Ms. Samantha's desk was empty. The headmistress' inner office door was open a crack and we wasted no time crossing the floor.

The screen from Headmistress Valentine's laptop cast her face with an eerie glow, highlighting her long nose and pale skin against her dark hair. She snapped her head up from her work, like she'd just been caught forging passports. "Good evening," she said, covering the papers on her desk with her arm. "It's late, is everything okay?"

Her eyes lit on me.

"You can't make Ms. Krick a student," I blurted out.

Valentine stared blankly at me, her eyes wide.

"Ava, discussions have been ongoing," she managed to say, after a beat, then put the cap on her pen. "Matilda agrees it's time. She had quite a scare tonight. And you are…?" She smiled at Dad.

"I'm Ava's father," he said, holding his ground. "I was a student of Ms. Krick's. I've known her a long time. It would be very dangerous to make her a student."

"Oh?" Valentine's smile turned up at the corners. She was amused. Or at least intrigued. "Matilda is insisting that the certificate for her day as a student be perfect. It's what I'm working on now." She moved her arm to reveal a paper trimmed with an elaborate blue border and a seal affixed to the bottom corner.

"I'll bet she is," Ethan mumbled under his breath.

"Are you offering to help with her farewell?" Valentine asked.

My chest tightened at the suggestion. She was being deliberately dense. Sarcastic even. We were unwelcome intruders, although she forced a smile.

"Sorry to interrupt, headmistress." Dad cleared his throat. "But this is a very serious matter."

"Did you want to give a tribute tomorrow?" Valentine sat back in her high-backed roller chair with her arms folded. She was toying with him now.

"No, no…" Dad trailed off.

"Did you tell her?" Courtney tripped on the threshold as she rushed into the headmistress' office, but Cole caught her arm to keep her from falling. He'd come with her. The wall of wishes, the fountain. They hadn't scared him off. Courtney's eyes darted wildly around the room.

"Not yet," I said, stepping up to Valentine's desk. "You can't make Ms. Krick an honorary student. She's Isaac Young's great-granddaughter. She wants to be a student to make a wish. You can't let that happen."

Ethan darted me a warning look. We hadn't exactly agreed on a plan of attack. My heart beat in my temples as Valentine's laughter rang through the office.

She tucked her hair behind her ears as she gained her composure. "I'm well aware of Ms. Krick's ramblings about wishes."

I breathed a sigh of relief. This was going to be more straightforward than I'd hoped.

"Although her relation to Mr. Young was a bit of a surprise, I only found that out tonight, after her outburst. The ink isn't dry yet, but it's done." She waved the certificate in front of her face.

"Ms. Krick wants to find the fountain. If she becomes a student, that will happen," Courtney said, in a rush.

Valentine trained her gaze on Courtney as though she'd only just noticed her arrival. She smoothed the certificate back onto the desk in front of her. "Ah, the fountain," the headmistress said. "And what, pray tell, does she plan to wish for?" She directed her question at Courtney.

The five of us looked between ourselves, searching for answers we didn't have. Valentine's sigh was laced with exasperation.

"We're not sure," I admitted.

"Well, I must say that I won't miss the ludicrous stories she invents." Valentine's tone was dismissive. "And the good people she convinces." Her disgust was directed at Dad.

"But the fountain is real," Ethan said slowly. "We've all seen it. Well, not Cole. Ava and Mr. Marshall have wished on it. Courtney, too." His assertion fell on Valentine's deaf ears. Her eyes crinkled at the corners. She was trying not to smile.

"And I've wished on many fountains in my day, Ethan," she said. "And nothing has ever come of it. If there were a fountain in the West Woods, which nobody has been able to find, Matilda Krick can wish to her heart's content on her last day on this property. And then she'll leave, for good, and we can go back to the business of learning." She clasped her hands on the desk in front of her. This meeting was over as far as she was concerned.

"Headmistress," said Dad. "You may not want to believe these kids, but believe me. There is a long tradition of strange things happening at this school. Building the road is a mistake. And letting Ms. Krick be a student for the day is a mistake too."

Headmistress Valentine tilted her head back and laughed. I bristled at her sharp peals. Dad really hadn't given her much to go on.

"Why not just fire her? Why agree to this at all?" I asked.

"I inherited Matilda as a teacher when I became headmistress of the school." Valentine let loose a heavy sigh. "And her antics aren't new, but she doesn't represent the future of St. Augustus. The deal for the road is none of her concern. It's between the mayor and the school. She can have whatever kind of party she wants on her way out the door." Headmistress Valentine stood. Cole shifted uneasily at the mention of his mother.

"Kids, it's time to go," Dad said, turning to usher us out. "We have work to do."

"Dad -" My protest was silenced by Dad's raised hand. And the wink he gave me. He was probably right. There was nothing more to be done here. Our appeal had been squashed like an ant under Valentine's heel.

"Will you be staying in the area long?" Valentine asked him, as he herded us toward the door.

"As long as I'm needed," Dad said, holding the door open for us to funnel out by ducking under his arm.

The stone corridor that had once been full of excitement closed in with gloom around us as we left the light of the main office. The hour was catching up to me.

"Sorry, kids," Dad said, as we trudged toward the foyer, his shoulders slumped. "I don't know what I was thinking. I've never tried to tell anyone about the fountain before. I guess I should have known how ridiculous it would sound."

"You didn't know, Dad." I patted his arm. My voice echoed in the cavernous room. The overhead chandeliers were dark, but emergency lamps at each end cast pools of light. We huddled together under one of the lamps. "And there are others who believed, even without any proof."

I caught Ethan's eye, a surge of gratitude flooding my senses. He'd been on my side, even before we discovered the wall of wishes. Before he'd had any reason to believe that my story about Courtney disappearing was true.

"Who would make up such an insane story about a mean girl who disappeared?" Ethan replied, laughing. "No offense, Courtney."

She grinned and shrugged. "None taken."

"Well, I don't know what to believe," Cole said, stuffing his hands in his pockets. "But walls don't usually project memories into your mind. That was real, right?"

"It was the alternate timelines. The ones affected by wishes on the fountain," I confirmed, shivering.

Ethan slipped his arm around my shoulders, spreading warmth. The images of every student who'd ever wished on the fountain hadn't left me. We had work to do if we were going to protect them and we only had that night.

"We may not be able to stop Ms. Krick from becoming a student," Cole said. "But we can apply to protect the graves." He ran his fingers along the stone lining the foyer, measuring, appraising.

"The fountain can be a lot to take in," Dad said. "And maybe from now on we shouldn't try to convince anyone else that it exists."

"I'd heard rumors of the magic on campus," Cole said, choosing his words slowly. "Mostly from my dad. And I can't say right now what I believe exactly, but that, whatever that was, it was something amazing. It deserves to be protected." A pink flush crept across his cheeks.

Dad frowned. "It's the weekend. No permit is going to get done tonight."

"I'll go to Ms. Krick. If we know what she's planning, we have a better chance of stopping her," Courtney said, rounding on me. "Ava, will you go with me?"

"I'm not exactly her favorite." My mouth twisted into a sideways smile. I was hoping to sleep at some point that night.

"Please," Courtney said.

"A-All right," I stammered.

One night of sleep wasn't worth risking my existence, where I'd never sleep again. My heart raced and I'd been pushed to the brink of exhaustion, but she was right. I could sleep tomorrow, when this was all over, one way or another. We had to find out Ms. Krick's plan.

"Well, she definitely hates me, so I should stay clear," Ethan said. "I'll go with Cole and Mr. Marshall and see if I can hack some permits into Evergreen's records or something."

"I can't condone that," Dad said, his frown deepening.

"He's kidding, Dad," I said, lacing my fingers through Ethan's. I'd seen few glimpses of Ethan's light-hearted joking in the previous few weeks. "But he's really good with computers. Give him something to do."

"Let's try to catch Ms. Krick at the teachers' residence," Courtney said. "She might be back by now."

"They gave her a sedative." I was skeptical they'd let her go home but then again, she wouldn't want to stay at Cole's once she woke. It was the eve of her big day.

"You saw the certificate," Courtney said. "She'll become a student at midnight."

It was like a reverse Cinderella story of sorts. I shivered. If Ms. Krick was Cinderella, what did that make us? The mice and the birds, running around trying to make things happen? My mind was starting to crack.

"I'm sending a note to the guy I worked with on the historical designation for the house," Cole said, tapping on his phone. "Most of the forms are online, but he can probably answer any questions we have. There might be something we can do tonight, if he's still up."

"Go find Ms. Krick," Dad urged me. "Tell her I say hi. Or, on second thought, maybe leave me out of it."

"She doesn't like you either?" Ethan asked him.

"I was never her favorite. But at least I'm in good company," Dad replied, smiling at Ethan. "Boys, come with me. My laptop is over at Gran's house, we can work on the application there."

Courtney took my arm and led me down the hall. I resisted the urge to pull away from her grasp. The wall had shown me more than her actions. Her pain had rolled through my gut as she'd tried to free herself from the fountain's clutches. My own heart ached with hers.

"Thank you." Courtney clutched my arm tightly as the cold night air hit us.

CHAPTER TWENTY

Courtney

I'd relived standing on the landing outside Ms. Krick's apartment when I'd touched the wall. I'd been here in another lifetime and seeing it play on the film reel the wall showed us sent my stomach into knots. I'd been a different person then and I didn't want to go back.

I shifted my weight from foot to foot as Ava and I stood on the landing, waiting. Ms. Krick's cat, Oscar, scratched at her apartment door from the inside. It could only be him. Her other cats were docile.

"Don't drink the tea if she offers it," I said to Ava, who fidgeted beside me.

I wouldn't blame her if she left me here, after everything I'd done to her. I'd wanted the freeway to pave over it all, to start again. But I'd only been thinking about myself. There were so many others who'd shared dreams and fears with the fountain, who'd been granted what was in their hearts. That had to be protected.

Despite my initial excitement for a clean slate, nothing good would come of undoing the past. The fountain's powers were far reaching. Ava owed her existence to it and I would help her fight. She shifted beside me as footsteps came from inside. Ms. Krick was home.

"Yes?" Ms. Krick opened the door only an inch, but it was enough to see her bare legs sticking out from a too-short St. Augustus kilt. Her shins sported a gray blanket of leg hair. "What do you girls want?"

"Are you wearing a school uniform?" Ava said, gaping.

Ms. Krick opened the door a little wider, revealing her lopsided kilt, stopping three inches above her knees. She wore a creased white St. Augustus blouse, complete with the likeness of Izzy on its crest.

"Didn't you hear?" Ms. Krick's frown deepened. "I'm going to be student for the day tomorrow. Everything has to be perfect. I need to borrow knee socks. Would one of you please bring me a pair?"

Ava's eyebrows shot up as we exchanged a look. Ms. Krick hadn't mentioned the late hour. She also hadn't questioned us being out alone in the middle of the night.

"That's why we're here," I said, thinking quickly. "We'd like to help you get ready."

"Oh?" Ms. Krick itched at her skirt. "Well, you can pack then."

"Pack?" Ava asked, craning her neck to see past the diminutive teacher into the cramped apartment.

"Sure," I said, pushing past her into her mustard-pickle scented lair.

Packing gave us an excuse to hang around and find out what she was up to. Stall her even.

"The school has given me until the end of the week to be out," Ms. Krick said, picking up a hissing Oscar, whose black fur stood on end.

Ava hung back by the door, her mouth hanging open. Everything was just as I remembered it, with stacks of papers and belongings lining the walls and multi-colored carpet sample squares covering the floors from end to end. I cringed as three of Krick's multitude of cats twined themselves around my legs. I waved for Ava to join me.

"Is this place for real?" she said, under her breath. "How did she start packing so fast?"

"It's always like this," I whispered back, surveying the piles in the darkened corners.

"I'll get the boxes." Ms. Krick disappeared into the back of the apartment.

"How is she even standing?" Ava asked. "When I left, she was sleeping."

I shrugged. Ms. Krick was determined, if nothing else.

"She isn't that broken up about leaving the school," Ava said, picking her way through Ms. Krick's mess. "Maybe we can get her talking."

"She collects things that were Isaac Young's," I said, picking my way toward a pile of binders. "If we can find one and ask her about it, we could steer the conversation."

Ava wrinkled her nose as she crouched beside a dusty stack of notebooks and flipped open the top one. "Ethan's description didn't do this apartment justice."

"You can start with these," Ms. Krick hugged a handful of large collapsed cardboard boxes against her, which dragged on the ground.

I rushed to her side. "Let me take those." I set the boxes on the ground. "But your hair won't do for a student. It isn't authentic." I clucked my tongue, shaking my head.

"Oh?" she asked, patting her French roll, which didn't show any sign of having been plunged in a lake earlier that evening.

Her place was like the twilight zone, where night felt like day.

"Do you have a hair tie? We could braid it," I said, pushing her by the shoulders toward the back of the apartment. I glanced over my shoulder at Ava, who'd moved on to a new stack. "Why don't you go find a brush and I'll help you."

"Any idea what we're looking for?" Ava asked, once Ms. Krick had disappeared.

"There was a map. My dad gave it to me once." I hesitated. Ava and I hadn't compared our experiences. It was strange to be telling her about my former life, the one she'd erased. But in this timeline, my dad had never gone to the school and couldn't have stolen the map from Ms. Krick's apartment. I pushed down the panic with which my brain tried to cloud my thinking. "It's on a wide piece of parchment, rolled up with an elastic around it."

"Maybe Ms. Krick could the elastic for her hair?" Ava quipped.

Her smile warmed me. She might never forgive me, but she was making an effort. I went to the window. Pronged tracks lined the flat roof a few feet below. Izzy had been there recently.

"Sadly, Izzy has abandoned me just as I am about to fulfill our family's destiny." Ms. Krick was right behind me. Her voice was wistful. My neck prickled. If he'd been here, Krick hadn't seen him.

"We'll help with your destiny," I said, patting her arm.

My heartbeat pounded in my ears. She was going to see right through my insincerity.

"I don't think I need to tell you of my great-grand-pappy's powers." Ms. Krick's voice dipped. Her eyes flashed at me. "He would want me to have them."

I withdrew my hand. My blood ran like ice under my skin. Isaac Young's power had created the fountain, the wall of wishes, and the magical map. Was there more? He'd given the fountain as a gift to the students, to support their dreams. It all became weapons in the wrong hands. Hands such as Ms. Krick's.

Ms. Krick clapped her hands together. "Those who have mocked me will be sorry. And there will be nothing they can do."

She was off her rocker that night, even more than usual.

Ava rose to her feet. "I forgot, I was supposed to meet Ethan," she said, dusting invisible grime off Cole's sweats that she still wore. Her eyes were as wild as Ms. Krick's. "Let's go, Courtney."

"What?" I mouthed to her.

We hadn't found what we needed. What was she doing? Ava jerked her head at the door. She wanted to go.

Ms. Krick bent to pick up Oscar, whispering into his ear. "Don't worry, I won't forget about you, Oscar," she said. She giggled into his fur, apparently forgetting we were even there. Perhaps the drugs they'd given her were still in her system. "You're coming with me."

"Good luck packing, Ms. Krick," I said, edging my way to the door.

Ava made a beeline to my side.

"She's completely lost her mind," Ava said as we crept down

the steep stairs of the teachers' residence. "I found this in one of her junk piles." She held up what looked like a smooth yellow stone. It was the same oval shape as the red one Cole's Dad had under glass in their dining room.

"It looks like the one at Cole's house. Do you know what they're for?" I asked as we let ourselves out of the teachers' residence.

Every door on the main floor was dark. The few teachers that lived in the place must be asleep.

"Ethan has a blue one. It calls Izzy if you rub it," she said. "That's why he brought us the pages from Isaac Young's missing journal."

"I'm starting to think Izzy is..." I couldn't finish the thought out loud. Even with everything going on, it was a stretch.

"Human?" Ava prompted.

"Yeah," I said.

We were on the same wavelength, whether it made sense or not. Izzy's mannerisms were precise, deliberate. It all fit. Ava saw it too. I'd stopped questioning what was possible around St. Augustus a long time ago.

She held the yellow stone out to me. It glowed faintly in her hand, although I couldn't be sure if it was from the stone itself, or just a reflection from the moonlight.

I took the stone from her and rubbed it.

The stars above us twinkled expectantly, but there was no sign of Izzy. The stone's glow faded as a cloud covered the moon, leaving the rock dull in my palm.

Ava pulled out her phone and scrolled through her messages.

"Shoot, we missed the boys," she said. "Dad sent them to bed." She exited her chat with Ethan and pulled up another. "My Dad wants us to meet at six tomorrow morning."

"You mean this morning," I corrected her. "It's after midnight."

I glanced back at the teachers' residence. Ms. Krick's lights still burned brightly in the top turret of the house.

"She's busy packing," Ava said, stifling a yawn. "She probably won't venture out tonight."

I caught her yawn, stretching my arms above my head. A few

hours sleep would do us both a lot of good. It had been a very long day.

"Let's hope six is early enough," I said.

CHAPTER TWENTY-ONE

Ava

I'd just drifted off to sleep when a handful of pebbles cracked against my window. I swung my legs over the side of my bed, shaking my head to get my bearings. I'd turned in wearing my own sweatpants and an St. Augustus T-shirt with Izzy's likeness silkscreened on the front. I was drenched in sweat. I'd been under deep. The clock said it was just after three. I pulled on my swim team hoodie and went to the window.

In the moonlight, Ethan's shadow wavered against thick snowflakes falling on the ground. I pushed open my window a smidge and a skiff of snow blew in. He waved for me to come down. I looked over at Jules, who rolled toward me in her single bed, her eyes cracking open.

"Can't you two just see each other in the morning?" She groaned and pulled her covers over her head. "Close the window."

I tugged the window shut, and pointed to the dorm's front entrance. I wasn't going out the window that night, I'd have to leave it open to get back and our room would fill with snow.

"It's important," I whispered to Jules. "I'll be back soon."

I grabbed a coat and pulled on my boots, which were almost dry. I was starting to get used to the Massachusetts weather again. I snatched Jules' beanie from the top of her dresser. It had her woolen mitts stuffed inside it, which I pulled on.

Jules grunted but didn't emerge from her cocoon as I closed our door behind me. The hall was silent, with only the emergency light glowing over the door to the bathroom. My temples throbbed with lack of sleep. I'd already missed curfew, but Jules told Bessie I was with my dad, so I'd probably get away with it. I'd been through so much I just couldn't muster any fear as I padded to the front door and let myself out. Wind whistled into the dorm's hall as I braced the door from the outside. My bones still ached from my earlier swim and lack of recovery time. When this was all over, I was going to sleep for a week.

"Sorry to wake you. I didn't think it could wait," Ethan called from the bottom of the snow-covered stairs. "It's tomorrow already and the thought of Ms. Krick…"

He didn't need to finish his sentence. The scenarios had run through my mind too, none of them good.

"Did you think of something?" I asked.

Short of physically barring her from the woods at sunrise, I'd come up empty.

"I still have a wish." Ethan rubbed his gloves together and let his words sink in. "And I want more than anything to keep her from the fountain."

Snowflakes landed inside my open mouth.

"I've gone over the options and of course I've thought of many other wishes I could make," he said. "Keeping Krick from the fountain makes the most sense, don't you think?"

He wanted my approval. Could I give it? There were so many things in the world to fix. It was a wasted wish but a safe one. Things would stay the same and if all went well, the road would be built somewhere else and the fountain would be there for next year's students and the students after that. The thought of countless careless future wishes by teens coming through the campus left me colder than the flurries around me. The fountain was a miracle, the most dangerous miracle I could imagine.

I joined him at the bottom of the steps, nodding silently. How many more times would we have to make this thankless trek into the woods?

"Let's go," I said.

The sooner we went, the sooner I could get back to my warm bed. It wasn't a perfect solution, not a perfect wish, but it would buy us time. Yet, something nagged me.

"You can't come," Ethan said.

I looked up. "What?" I said.

But he was right and I knew it, even as he said it. If I went with him, the fountain wouldn't appear. I'd made a wish. I couldn't see the fountain anymore, it was invisible to me.

"I'll come with you to the edge of the woods," I said. "I'll wait there." I wouldn't be any help and we both knew that. Still, I'd feel better being nearby.

I took his hand and we started on the path toward the West Building. Months earlier, the thought of breaking a rule had made my heart race. That night, the only person that might be outside was Ms. Krick but she no longer made my pulse quicken. Her base desire to find the fountain was childish, even naïve. A pang of pity hit me. She'd be up early on her day as a student. That is, if she'd gone to bed at all. She'd already been dressed, without any knee socks to complete her uniform. I imagined her disappointment at finding that the clearing was just that – a clearing.

"Will you say, 'I wish for the fountain to not appear for Ms. Krick?'" I asked.

Ethan would have to choose his words carefully. There could be no loopholes. I turned the possibilities over in my mind. Was this wish foolproof?

"I was thinking that the fountain could still appear, but I could ask it not to grant Ms. Krick a wish. I think it's kinder somehow."

I rolled his idea over in my mind. If he worded it that way, Ms. Krick would see the fountain, confirming its existence. But her wish wouldn't work, which was the only thing that mattered. She didn't have any business making a wish. It was for students.

The sharp realization of how juvenile my own wish had been tore through me. I'd wished for Courtney and her family to be banished from St. Augustus' history. I'd been selfish and almost ruined everything for Courtney.

Except, I'd given her exactly what she'd wanted, a new start. The irony of it left my head spinning.

This snow didn't crunch under our feet. It was soft and fluffy. It covered the ground with a fresh start, where we could write our names, or leave it blank. It was a fresh layer of choices.

"How close do you think you can get without the fountain disappearing?" Ethan asked.

"I'll wait right over there, under the trees." I pointed to the edge of the woods, where an umbrella of evergreen boughs kept the ground relatively bare. He walked me there, then turned to face me.

"Ava, I've never felt more like myself than when I'm with you," he said.

My heart leaped. His words were a goodbye, of sorts. What did he think might happen? His fear rippled up my arms, restricting my chest. He'd never wanted to make a wish. This was a big deal for him.

"Me too," I said. And I meant it. I wasn't responsible for the whole mess the fountain had put us in, but I had set parts of it in motion. And he was about to use his wish to prevent Ms. Krick from unleashing more of the fountain's power.

"And I want us to have a chance," he said. "I'll wait for you to be ready. This has been a crazy year so far. Once it settles down..." He brushed a smattering of snow from my shoulders. I'd never wanted to push him away but time was short and the fountain still had a hold on me.

"I don't want to wait, I-" I said, blinking away the snow as my eyelashes fluttered against stray flakes that had turned to ice droplets.

Ethan leaned in and our cold lips touched. I wrapped my arms around his neck and let his kiss warm me from my core outward. It was our first real kiss since the night we'd found the wall of wishes and he'd told me how he felt. Since then we'd been on some kind of hold, where I'd let my feelings sit and wait, pushed them down.

His arms around my waist pulled me to him.

"Thank you for using your wish," I said, pulling back a little.

"If I could do more, I would," he said.

"You're going to stop Ms. Krick," I said, brushing my mitt against his cheek, which was red from cold. "I don't think the world's ready for whatever she's planning."

"I'll be right back and we can pick up where we left off." Ethan kissed my cheek then grinned as he pulled off his glove to fish a quarter out of his pocket. He held it up into the falling snow as he stepped out from under the tree's canopy. "This is the lucky coin." He pressed it to his lips.

"It looks lucky," I said, stamping my feet to stay warm.

He flashed me his widest smile, then jogged into the trees, toward the clearing. He ducked his head to avoid the branches overhead without breaking stride. In a few minutes, it would be done and nothing Ms. Krick could do would change things.

I hugged myself and stepped out into the open, letting the snow fall on my upturned face. We were out in the middle of the night, something I never would have done before meeting Ethan. And I was more alive than I'd ever been. I twirled slowly in a circle. Dad even liked Ethan. I looked forward to the day we didn't have to sneak out at night, when our lives would be normal. Ordinary.

"Ava!" a voice called from the campus lawn.

I squinted through the snow, where two figures took shape as they approached. Courtney and Cole were bundled up, hurrying my way. Courtney held something up in the air. Had I been the only one who'd gone to bed? They were both out of breath when they reached me.

"Where's Ethan?" Courtney asked.

I shrugged. "He went to use his wish." We were well beyond keeping secrets from one another. "He's going to block Ms. Krick."

"He still has a wish?" Courtney's eyes went wide. "We still might need it. We have to stop him!" She plunged into the trees, but Cole caught the back of her jacket.

"It's dark in there," he said. "We can all go together, right Ava?"

I had my phone out, dialing his number as I picked my way over the tree roots. He'd only get one wish. There wasn't time to find out their idea before trying to stop him.

"It went straight to voicemail," I called over my shoulder, stuffing my phone back into my pocket. "Ethan!" I cupped my hands around my mouth, calling his name into the woods.

"We think we know how to call Isaac Young to us," Courtney said from behind me. "We need all three stones."

My heartbeat quickened. She hadn't said they wanted to call Izzy to us. She said Isaac Young, like, his spirit.

Ethan would be at the clearing by now. If Courtney could talk to Isaac Young's spirit, we might get a better idea exactly what Ethan should wish to fix this mess. My blood ran cold. I smacked my forehead. It was so obvious I couldn't believe I hadn't thought of it before.

"He's like a genie," I said to Courtney, who was closest to me.

She blinked at me like I'd gone mad. Perhaps I had. Isaac Young was trapped inside an owl's body just like a genie was trapped in a bottle. If we could get him out, he could help us.

"Ethan!" I called ahead.

"I'm over here!" Ethan came crashing through the trees. "Look who I found."

My dad was right behind him, prodding a wild-eyed Ms. Krick, dressed in our school uniform, still minus the socks, in front of him.

My heart sank. We were too late. Ms. Krick had already been to the fountain.

"Dad, what are you doing here?" My head spun as I tried to work it out. Only the tip of Ms. Krick's red nose peeked over the woolly scarf wrapped around her face. Her eyes shot daggers at us all.

"It's past midnight," Dad said. "I know I told you kids to go to bed, but I didn't actually think she'd wait until dawn," Dad said, with a lopsided grin.

My heart sank. "Did she find the fountain?" I asked.

"So, you admit it's in there!" Ms. Krick's muffled voice exclaimed triumphantly. "I knew it! And I have a full twenty-four hours. You won't be able to stop me. I'll call the police."

"If I stay in the clearing, you'll never see it," Dad said, crossing his arms. "And you can't stop me from staying there. It's practically on my wife's family's land."

He was right. He'd used his wish and he was no longer a student, two things that made the fountain shy. As long as he was there, it wouldn't appear.

"Mariam? Ha." Ms. Krick glared at Dad. "She wouldn't have married you without the fountain's help, that's for sure. Did you ever tell her what you did?"

Dad's face went dark in the moonlight. "Leave my wife out of it." A low growl came from his throat.

My heart went to him. His pain was clear on his face, begging me. I moved to his side. "Dad. Mom loved wishing on fountains. She would have understood."

"You think so?" he said, almost choking on his words.

Ethan stepped forward from the shadows. "She knew," he said.

"What?" I stared at him. How could he possibly know that?

"Mariam. It was in her diary, the summer after she and your dad graduated," he said. "She'd been to the wall. She read Mr. Marshall's wish. She wrote about it. She was glad. She was happy."

Dad cocked his head to one side. His smile swirled with confusion. "Happy?"

"She said it was amazing that the fountain brought you together." Ethan patted him on the back.

I stared at Ethan. He'd read my mother's diaries. I'd never bothered to read them through. Why hadn't he said anything?

"She said you were both lucky to have a bond that would never be broken. I'm sorry, Ava, I thought you'd read the diaries. I thought you knew."

I shook my head, processing what he'd said.

"Yes, yes, but nobody cares about their measly love affair," Krick scoffed. "Some of us have more important wishes to make."

My mother had known all along. She loved fountains. And she'd forgiven Dad, seen his wish as a positive, even. She would have never allowed Ms. Krick to gain the fountain's power.

"What are you going to wish?" I demanded of Ms. Krick.

There would be time to sort through the rest later. Horror pricked at my neck again but she was confident enough. She might just admit it. Ms. Krick mumbled something unintelligible, then turned back toward the center of the woods.

"If we all go to the clearing, the fountain can't appear," Courtney called, thrashing ahead through the underbrush, with Cole by her side.

A ledge of snow overhead slid off a branch, splattering a pile at our feet.

"And thank you for confirming the fountain's location!" Ms. Krick's cackle was clear in the night air. "This day is getting better every moment. I could get used to being a student." Her gait was nimbler than her age should allow as she hastened away from us, her skirt flapping up and down as she walked. Wasn't she cold? She was only wearing a blouse and a school cardigan. Her legs were bare.

Ethan was hot on her heels, with Dad and I not far behind.

"Did you get to it? Did you make your wish?" I called to Ethan as we ran.

"Not yet," Ethan said, shaking his head as he slowed to let me catch up. "Your dad was in the clearing, waiting for Ms. Krick who arrived just after me. The fountain wasn't there. I'm sorry."

"No, that's good!"

He hadn't made his wish. I didn't have much time to catch him up to speed. There was another way. "Do you have Ms. Krick's stone?" I asked.

"Yes." He patted his coat pocket as we jogged side by side. "I keep it with me."

We burst into the clearing. Ms. Krick stood where the fountain should be. She swung her head from side to side. "Where is it?"

I ignored her. "Courtney and I found another one," I said, producing the amber stone we'd found in Ms. Krick's apartment and showing it to Ethan. Its faint glow had returned, hovering in an arc around the stone like a halo.

"And Cole and I went to get his dad's stone," Courtney said, gesturing to Cole, who held the red stone out.

"Should we try it now?" I asked.

"Yes," she said. "Ms. Krick has as much right to see him as the rest of us."

She was right. Ms. Krick was a direct descendant of Isaac Young. Conjuring him was a long shot. We'd be more likely to succeed with her there.

"Hold them all together, so they're touching," I instructed. Truth be told, I had no idea whether it would work, it was just a hunch.

"Here." Cole tossed his stone to Ethan, who caught it easily. The blue, yellow, and red stones sat in the palm of his gloved hand.

"Hey, those are mine!" Ms. Krick screeched as she lurched toward Ethan. Dad held her back with one arm.

"Steady, Krick." Dad's voice was firm.

Ethan frowned at the stones. They sat dull in his hand, their softly curved sides touching.

My stomach was in knots.

"It should have worked," Courtney whispered.

It had been a wild guess, at best, that putting them together would do something more fantastic than bringing Izzy the owl to us.

"Something's happening. I can feel it." Ethan's glove shook like a leaf, as a low rumble rippled under our feet. Ms. Krick gave a small hop, letting out a squeak like she'd stepped on a snake spiked with nails. A golden aura enveloped Ethan like a faded spotlight shining down from the trees. In his leather glove, the stones glowed, engulfing his hand, blinking like a beacon. A deep shadow fell over us all as swooping wings soared above the trees, circling to land his short brown-feathered body on spindly claws.

"It's only Izzy," I said. While I was glad to see that he hadn't been caught, my stomach churned. I don't know what else I expected.

We'd called Izzy before with only the blue stone. Three glowing stones should do something spectacular. I turned away. Courtney's idea of calling Isaac Young himself had planted itself like a seed in my mind, germinating until I believed it would happen. How had I let myself believe something so ridiculous? I shuddered. Disappointment settled around me like a cloak. Izzy's white-tipped feathers reflected the stone's frosty light.

The owl cocked his head at us, blinking his ghoulish stare. It was still the middle of the night and we were no further ahead. He couldn't talk.

"What do you know?" I asked Izzy. There was an edge to my voice but I didn't care. I'd nearly drowned only hours earlier and the carnival had been a bust. Dad and Cole had filled out online paperwork, but there was no guarantee it would work and at any rate the process would be slow. My legs were weak. My body was starting to shut down. I needed sleep.

Izzy blinked again.

I turned away as a sob spiraled up my throat and my shoulders shook. I closed my eyes and drew in a long breath through my nose. I blew the breath out through my mouth as the ground under my feet shuddered. A low rumble rippled up my legs, shooting up through my core. I turned around to see a tornado of light swirling around Izzy. The owl himself spun like a top, hovering several feet above the ground. I choked on my own gasp as he spun faster, his body elongating like stretching taffy as he turned.

"Stand back!" Dad cried out, pushing me away from Izzy's light.

Shards of sparks shot up into the trees like fireworks, crackling and sizzling in the branches of the trees overhead until they faded into a smattering of ash and rained down on us. Izzy was gone. Standing in his place in the snow was a man.

"It's him." Ms. Krick's gasp filled the clearing. In the middle of a bright circle of light stood a shimmering man with a kindly smile. I jumped back. I'd seen his face in our History class handouts, although he'd been in black and white. Standing before us was the floating image of Isaac Young in full color, complete with three-piece suit and bowtie.

"What have we done?" Dad said, clapping a hand over his mouth.

Ms. Krick fell to her knees, bowing to her ancestor in child's pose, with her kilted bottom poking up and her hands stretched in front of her. Ethan was frozen to the spot, his eyes as wide as mine. He still held the stones in his hand. Their light had gone out, but their colors had deepened.

"I have waited a long time to be called." Isaac's voice was as deep as the night. It boomed through the clearing. His waistcoat shimmered with stardust.

"Great Grand-Pappy!" Ms. Krick said. "You've come to help me. I have waited patiently to inherit your powers." Her eyes squeezed tight and she extended her arms as if she expected power to surge into her.

Isaac's gaze swept past Ms. Krick, resting on us all. "Are you all seeking power?" His frown deepened.

"No. We want to stop the road," Courtney blurted. "The students' wishes, they must be preserved."

Isaac Young's translucent eyes still glowed yellow like his owl form, reflecting his sadness. "I only ever wanted to help students find their way." He shook his head back and forth. "The fountain, it grew a life of its own." He held out an outstretched palm and a shadow emerged in the center of the clearing. It was black at first then shimmered into the marble blocks making up the fountain. It was just as I remembered it. A spring welled up inside me. I'd dreamed of the fountain many times since I'd first seen it.

"Woah." Cole rushed to the fountain's basin, stretching his hands to the rushing water, which bubbled through its pipes, spurting out to create half a dozen waterfalls. "It's real."

"It sure is." Courtney grinned beside him.

Her relief resonated deep within me. I stretched for Ethan's hand, which still held the stones.

"It's taking everything I have to hold their weight." He nodded at his hands. His eyes found mine. I cupped my hands around his, feeling the weight of the rocks push against us.

"Matilda, I'm sorry not to have known you," Isaac Young said, waving for her to rise, although she only straightened up, remaining on her knees. "I thank you for the great care you've taken of me in my owl form. I couldn't have asked for more but my magic will not help you find happiness. It's time you spread your wings, away from St. Augustus and stop chasing the past."

Ms. Krick's jaw hung open like she'd been slapped.

"The rest of you are on the right track," he said, his praise raining down on our shoulders, lifting my spirits. "If I could do it all again, I would have never created the fountain."

His gaze burned through each of us in turn as moments

passed under his watchful stare. My biceps trembled from the strain of the stones we still held. We couldn't let them drop. They'd brought Isaac Young to us. He had the power to stop the road and the power to keep my dad's wish intact. The power could freeze the present as it was. I hung on his every word.

"Every one of you has lost greatly because of my dream," he said.

My arms burned from the rocks' weight. "They're heavy. A little help?" I pleaded with the others.

They jumped in to help Ethan and me, all except Ms. Krick, who inched closer to Isaac Young's image, staring at him in wonder. Dad, Ethan, Courtney, Cole, and I were hunched over now, our backs bowed under the weight of the stones. Five pairs of our hands were nearly on the ground. Would Isaac Young disappear if we dropped them?

Isaac Young's extremities, clear as day moments before, had faded to foggy shapes. I bored all of my concentration into my hands.

"You've paid with your tears, with your worries," he continued. "The fountain mustn't be allowed to continue. You mustn't allow it to continue."

Pressure burned against my palms like fire. He wasn't done talking. He hadn't fixed anything yet.

The stones were like huge anvils of iron, attracted to the gravity of the Earth. Our hands all dropped at once as the weight became unbearable and the stones fell to the ground. I fell back into a snow drift with a wave of relief. The stones had fallen in a triangle pattern in front of me, their dark shapes dull against the white snow. I panted for air.

"Destroy the fountain!" Isaac Young's voice rang through the clearing as his body exploded into a million points of light, dispersing into a thin cloud hovering over the fountain. Its glow burned to the back of my retinas. I raised a hand to shield my eyes. The fountain's white marble had become translucent, fading quickly.

Courtney surged to the fountain's edge, but she was too late. With a quiver, the fountain shivered into the fog, eluding her grasping hands. It was gone, but not in a shower of light like Isaac Young had gone. The stone had just faded into the background, lying in wait as it always did. It would be visible again when the conditions were right, I felt sure of it.

Tears pricked at my eyes. A blanket of silence covered us all. I sat in the snow, unable to move, unable to speak. Isaac Young was gone, replaced by a flurry of fresh snow, driving down onto the stunned bunch of us.

"Kids, it's awfully late." I'd forgotten Dad was there. He stood with his hands limply at his sides, defeated. Destroying the fountain would undo everything. Undo *us*. I picked up the three perfectly oval stones. Even in the dim light, I could see that their color had drained. They were ordinary. I tossed them lightly. They were no longer heavy.

"The wishes," Dad said, standing where the fountain had been, staring at the back of his own hand. "They haven't been undone, yet."

"Dad, I..." I wasn't sure what I wanted to say to him, not exactly.

"I like my job," he said, looking up at the rest of us.

I'm not sure what I expected him to say, but that wasn't it.

"And Mia and Chuck's house is my home. Our home."

I accepted Ethan's hand to help me out of the snow bank. Dad's acceptance settled into my bones. Ethan and I stood so close our hips touched.

"I'm happy I met you, before," Cole said to Courtney, taking her hands. "And I'm happy to have this second chance, one that I won't take for granted."

Courtney beamed.

A stifled sob came from the ground near the edge of the clearing. Ms. Krick lay huddled, her shoulders shaking with grief.

Ethan and I scurried over to her. I slipped the stones into the pocket of Ethan's coat as I crouched at her side.

"We'll help you get back to your residence," Ethan said, offering her his arm.

"Great Grand-Pappy knew me," she said, through her sobs. "All I ever wanted was my birthright. And he knows me. He said my name."

I could only stare. Her obsession. All these years, it hadn't been about the fountain. Ethan and I helped her to her feet.

"It's time we all got some sleep," Dad said. "Ava, will you come to Gran's?"

I shook my head. "I belong on campus, Dad." Nothing had been resolved, but I had no strength left. I wanted my own bed.

"I suppose you do," he said, smiling. "I'll walk you all back."

We fell into line. Ethan and I supported Ms. Krick's sobbing mess, Courtney and Cole held hands, and Dad brought up the rear. Ms. Krick's shoulders curled in as she muttered to herself, lifting her loafer-clad feet with every step.

As we passed under the canopy of branches, the night closed in around us. The moonlight was drowned out.

"He disappeared into smoke," Ms. Krick mumbled as she trudged along, leaning her weight on us. With any luck, she'd sleep her way through her day as an honorary student.

The fountain had faded in the clearing, but Isaac Young hadn't destroyed it. We had to assume it would still appear if a student hadn't yet made a wish. If Ms. Krick went to the clearing while she was an honorary student, she'd still get to make her wish. Dad couldn't stand guard until midnight. We all needed rest.

"He told us to stop the fountain," Courtney said, as though she read my mind. "But we don't know how to stop it."

Her despair rattled through me but I found I *did* know how to stop it. The answer had been there all along. "Ethan," I whispered over Ms. Krick's head. I let go of her, leaving Ethan to support her full weight. I scurried around to his other side and whispered in his ear. His spine straightened.

"Are we therrrre yet?" Ms. Krick slurred her words.

"Of course," Ethan replied, as our gazes locked.

"We are?" Ms. Krick looked at us, or right through us. Her eyes were cloudy.

"Yes, yes. Ava will get you home." Ethan patted her back, then gently removed her arm from around his shoulders and draped her over me. "Mr. Marshall, would you help Ava get Ms. Krick home?"

Dad joined us, taking Ms. Krick's other arm. "Where are you going?" he asked Ethan.

"Dad, he can fix this," I said. I couldn't say it out loud. I didn't want to jinx his chances. "Trust us."

Ethan squeezed my arm and leaned in to kiss my cheek, then dropped into the peripheral trees. The warmth from his kiss lingered, chasing away the veil of exhaustion I'd worn all night. I could stay up for days if I knew our futures, our pasts, were safe. Letting him walk away from me was the only way that could happen.

Courtney and Cole talked quietly, huddled together. Courtney was pretty when she smiled. They didn't ask where Ethan had gone, but his absence tugged keenly at me.

"He's my Great-Grand Pappy," Ms. Krick said, smiling at me.

"Yes, and he knew you," I said.

Dad and I exchanged a look. The ice crunched under every careful step we took, dragging her with us. Ms. Krick needed medical attention. She'd been through a lot. Perhaps too much. Dad reached for his phone.

"He did." Ms. Krick nodded her head in satisfaction. Her goofy grin unnerved me.

We reached the edge of the trees, spilling out onto the lawn as one clump.

Dad had his phone to his ear. "Yes, we have a teacher at St. Augustus who is disoriented. She had mild hypothermia last night, and I just found her wandering on the lawn. Please come to the teachers' residence."

I took off my jacket and put it over Ms. Krick's back. "We have to go," I said, taking Courtney's hand. "Can you get home okay?" I asked Cole.

He nodded.

Dad was off the phone. "None of you can be here when the ambulance arrives," he said. "I'll wait with her. And Ethan…"

"He'll be fine, Dad," I said. "He knows his way around the campus at night." That probably wasn't what I should tell Dad about my boyfriend, but it was true.

"Come with me, Ms. Krick," Dad said, picking her frail body up in his arms.

She was still smiling.

"She's so confused they won't believe anything she says," he said. "And they'll hopefully keep her at the hospital at least for today. Tomorrow, her status as a student will be expired."

"I'm a student!" Ms. Krick declared, patting her skirt.

Dad ignored her, as we heard the faint sound of sirens in the background.

"Go," Dad urged us. "And don't come out. I'm going to say I found her wandering near Gran's. I'll leave you all out of it."

"Get some sleep," Cole said to Courtney, giving her a quick hug.

"Text me when you get home," Courtney said.

"Definitely," he said, winking at her. He turned and sprinted across the lawn without looking back.

The sirens were getting louder.

"Go," Dad said.

Courtney squeezed my hand then dropped it. We sprinted side by side across the lawn to the dorm stairs. I didn't stop until I closed the door to my room behind me.

"Everything okay?" Jules' sleepy voice asked. "What's going on?"

"Never better," I said.

Our window looked out over the lawn, which was bathed in a red glow, coming from the street. The West Woods beyond pulsed with each turn of the ambulance's light. There was no sign of Ethan.

Jules joined me at the window. She had her comforter pulled tightly around her shoulders. "Is that smoke?" she asked, pointing to the sky.

I was filled with hope, spreading to my fingertips. Above the woods, a giant plume of pink smoke billowed like a parachute, fluttering its gentle wisps in the air. It was done. There was nothing sinister about it. Ethan would be fine but the fountain would not. I would never see it again and neither would anybody else.

CHAPTER TWENTY-TWO

Ava

"She said yes!" Courtney's curls came bounding down the hallway of the newly minted clubs house, converted from the now vacant teachers' residence. Over the summer, the old apartments had been turned into a series of rooms where teams and clubs could gather. It was going to be an amazing senior year.

Courtney nearly knocked me down with a bear hug as I fit my shiny metal key into the lock of the swim team's door. I laughed as her arms crushed around my ribs.

"What's all the commotion?" Jules popped her head out from across the hall, the home to the new cheer team's head office. Their door was painted with silver glitter.

"Coach Laurel agreed to let us be co-captains of the swim team this year," Courtney said, holding a black plaque with both our names on it.

My chest puffed at the sight of our names linked. It would have been impossible to decide which of us deserved it more and we'd agreed not to compete. The job belonged to both of us, in any timeline.

Jules laughed. "Aren't you two going to be sick of each other, rooming together and running a team?" She popped a bubble with her gum.

Courtney and I shared a grin. Getting sick of each other wasn't likely. Our secrets made even the silent times we spent together comforting. Courtney had even spent two weeks with me and my dad in San Francisco over the summer, in Dad's new condo, a separate space from Mia and Chuck. It had an outdoor swimming pool long enough for laps. Courtney was faster than me now at the crawl, but I had her beat at breaststroke. New beginnings were everywhere that fall.

"How is your Gran adjusting?" Jules asked me.

Gran had gifted her house to the school, for teachers to live in, under the condition that the old teachers' residence be given to the students as a gathering place. It had all been Dad's idea, fueled by Jules' explanation of her vision for the clubs' space.

"I visited her this morning," I said. "Her retirement home has activities every day. She's learned to play bridge. I've never seen her so happy."

"Jules, did you get paired with a roommate?" Courtney asked.

She'd just arrived on campus. I'd arrived a few hours before.

It had been a difficult conversation, when I'd called Jules to tell her that Courtney and I planned to room together in the fall, but she'd been great, as Jules always was.

"I'm by myself," she grinned. "I won't miss Ethan's late-night rocks trying to break our window."

"Are you ladies all standing around talking about me?"

My breath caught as Ethan's familiar voice sent joy through my core.

"Ethan!" I ran to him and jumped up with my legs around his waist. He twirled me around twice then set me on my feet, planting his sorely missed kiss on my lips. We'd talked or texted every night over the summer months while he was a counselor at a summer camp in Maine, but I hadn't had his arms around me since we'd left campus in June. I snuggled in, tucking my chin into his chest. I couldn't get close enough to him, although Jules clearing her throat loudly made me come to my senses. Ethan and I parted a few inches, with me smiling so wide my teeth hurt.

"Some things never change," Jules said, laughing.

But so much had changed. And Jules had no idea.

"This place is amazing," Ethan said, looking around at the long hallway filled with doors. "Lots of mischief to be made in these halls." He rubbed his hands together. I groaned. We'd had enough adventure to last a lifetime. I was actually looking forward to a quiet year with my friends.

"Your swim team door is too bare," Jules said, ducking back behind the cheer team's silver door.

"Coach Laurel said yes?" Ethan asked, nodding to the plaque in Courtney's hands with our names on it.

"Mm-hmm," I said, hugging him again.

Everything was how it should be.

"Your door needs glitter." Jules emerged holding two pots of paint.

Courtney smiled wide and I beamed back, except she wasn't looking at me.

"Hello, Mr. Historian," she said.

Cole stood behind us, holding a large file folder sheepishly. "Can you show me where these go?" he asked.

Courtney swept past us, taking his arm and leading him to the back of the building. They'd been back and forth from Evergreen to Boston several times over the summer to spend time together.

"I've got this, you go." Jules set her paints on the floor. She shooed us to follow Cole, as I gave her a grateful smile.

"Did you really have to sit down with Ms. Krick?" Ethan asked Cole as we all climbed the first set of stairs.

While he'd been at his summer job, Cole had lobbied the city to document St. Augustus' past. He and Dad had worked long-distance together to support their bid to have Isaac Young's house and grave declared a landmark and they'd succeeded. Their initial application had put a stay on the road plans and the whole project had been called off at the end of August. Senator Wallis' inquiry exposed the questionable taxes the school had been forced to pay. The city had refunded the previous years' overpayments, some of which Valentine had redirected reluctantly to our new clubs' house, under direct pressure from Courtney's dad.

The second-floor of the clubs' house was abuzz with activity. Music pumped through the hall, and Jules' cheer teammates were busy painting all the other doors with bright colors. I laughed. It had been Jules' idea. It was only fitting that her style should be spread around.

"Matilda is actually fascinating," Cole said, blushing to the roots of his hair. "She's got an eye for historical detail. She gave us all of this to display, so don't be too hard on her."

I cringed at his use of Ms. Krick's first name. She'd never be anything but Krick to me. We climbed single file up the winding stairs to the top apartment. It was the apartment Ms. Krick, her cats, and her collection of junk and papers used to call home. After our encounter with Isaac Young in the woods, Krick had spent a week in the hospital. Her day as a student had been delayed instead of canceled, but of course the fountain was gone when the time finally came around. Ethan had seen to that.

Still, once Dad and Cole had asked Krick if she'd be willing to share her collection, she'd jumped in, generously giving what she'd amassed over the years to protect her great grand-pappy's legacy. His recognition of her had changed her. Somehow it seemed to be enough.

Cole had thrown himself into the project wholeheartedly, saying it was the least he could do, considering how his dad's fascination with destroying the woods had nearly cost the school everything. "Isaac Young's dream shouldn't be forgotten," he'd said. "That's what historical preservation is all about."

The four of us piled up at the landing at the top of the back stairs.

"This is her old apartment?" Cole asked.

Courtney nodded, touching the bronze knocker shaped like a small owl. I half expected to hear Ms. Krick's cat, Oscar, screeching inside. Instead, the door squeaked on its hinges as Courtney opened it. The colorful scraps of carpet covering the floors were gone. Only a whiff of the apartment's former musty existence lingered in the air. A few walls had been removed and the wooden floors refinished. The whole place was spotless and white, creating an airy study lounge.

Ms. Krick's cat-hair coated couches had been replaced with four long tables, lined with chairs. I scuffed the gleaming hardwood under my feet with my runner. The transformation was complete. Any trace of her was gone.

"I would even drink tea from this kitchen," Courtney said, twirling with her arms wide in the sparkling galley that had been completely gutted.

In place of Ms. Krick's cramped kitchenette were a white tiled floor, shiny stainless-steel appliances, and glossy white countertops.

"We can lock the papers in here until we're ready." Courtney opened a cupboard that had a key sticking out of a lock. Cole put his files on the counter, sorting them into piles before neatly stacking them on the shelf. The plan was to frame some of the memorabilia to decorate the space as a tribute to Isaac Young and Ms. Krick.

Ethan docked his phone on a sound station set up by the windows, tuning it to his upbeat playlist.

"Krick *did* have the map," Courtney said, plucking a roll of parchment out of Cole's bundle. She rolled off the elastic band holding it together and held it toward the window.

"I wanted that one to be a surprise," Cole said. "But I tested it with the sunlight like you described. It doesn't work anymore."

Courtney shook her head. "It only works at sunrise."

"None of the magic works anymore, remember?" I reminded her, placing a hand on her arm.

"Matilda thinks it's because Isaac Young left," Cole said, chuckling at her mistake.

"Perfect, let her think that." Ethan grinned.

He'd been the one to bind the fountain's powers. In the process, all the magic at the school had been snuffed out. The wall of wishes was still under the trees, but no new wishes would be added. And touching it did nothing. Our school seemed ordinary. Yet everyone in the room knew it wasn't.

"What exactly did you say for your wish?" Courtney asked Ethan. "I never asked."

Ethan cleared his throat. His eyes darted to the door. But we were the only ones here. "I wish to protect every wish ever granted on this fountain as is, and for no more to ever be granted," he said.

I mouthed the words with him as he said them. I'd thought about it many times since he'd told me what he'd wished that night. I'd had the idea to use his wish to bind the fountain's past and future, but his choice of words was perfect. They ensured our past. Our future.

"You didn't just wish for the fountain to disappear?" Courtney asked, scrunching up her nose. "I thought you had. Do you think it could still come back? It was invisible before. How would we know?" She looked at each of us in turn.

"After my wish, the fountain turned into pink smoke, just like I told you," he said, shrugging.

"I saw that from the dorm," I added.

"I guess it's possible it would come back, but I don't think so," Ethan said. "I think it's gone."

"We've each made a wish, except for Cole, who isn't a student," I said. "So, we have no way of checking."

"Actually..." Cole trailed off, smiling.

"You got in?" Courtney squealed, wrapping her arms around him.

I caught Ethan's eye and the two of us laughed.

"I'm going to be a senior at St. Augustus," Cole announced. "Mom and Dad didn't agree to let me live in the dorms, but at least we'll have some classes together."

I blinked in surprise. Given his parents' actions against the school, his attending was the last thing I expected.

Cole laughed at the expression on my face. "I know. Ms. Krick won't forgive my dad either and I don't expect you to, although he loves this town and the folklore of the school. I have him convinced he was chasing urban legends all this time. Besides, my mom was accused of hating St. Augustus, because of the taxes and all, which were my dad's idea. He was trying to gain control of the woods, to find the same thing Krick was chasing, I suppose. Sending me here is just good optics for Mom's re-election next year."

"Your door's done!" Jules burst into the bright space, wiping glitter from her cheek. "Nice tunes you've got going here. I painted a mermaid. You should go see. Because swimmers are beautiful creatures." She smiled.

"Perfect," I said. Whatever she'd put on our door would be perfect. Jules had a knack.

"I'm hosting a welcome party in my new room tonight at nine," Jules said. "You girls had better be there!" She wagged a mock-stern finger at us.

"We wouldn't miss it," I answered for both of us.

"Sorry Ethan, Cole," she said. "No boys allowed."

They laughed.

"What room are you in?" I asked. Courtney and I had kept the room Jules and I had shared the year before.

"Ooh," Jules said, clapping her hands together. "I didn't tell you the best part. I'm in room sixty-five, the *lucky* room. You're looking at a girl who's about to have a charmed year." She flipped her thick dark hair behind her shoulder as she danced her way out of the room, leaving the flowered scent of her shampoo in her wake. A room always felt emptier after Jules left it and this one was no exception. The four of us burst into laughter when she'd gone.

"Poor Jules," I said, shaking my head. We'd discovered the year before that the lucky room gave students dreams that helped them find the fountain.

"There's nothing lucky about the room anymore," Courtney said, grinning.

The magic that had charmed that room had probably been snuffed out like all the rest.

"Jules doesn't need luck," Ethan said, his hands on his hips. "She's Jules."

His light-hearted words sent us into fresh peals of laughter.

"Does school start today?" Cole asked. "I mean, I know classes don't start until tomorrow, but technically today is move-in day. Am I officially a student?"

What was he getting at? He was starting to sound like Ms. Krick.

"There's no harm in making sure," Courtney said, excitement behind her eyes. "He'll tell us once and for all if the fountain is gone. He's a student now and he hasn't made a wish. If anyone could see it, it would be him."

The two could be brother and sister, their complexions were so alike. They each grinned with wattage to match the other. They'd clearly planned this together but they wanted us to be part of the adventure.

"Let's go," Ethan said, gesturing to the door.

"Now?" Cole asked.

"Yeah, we like to dive into things. Welcome to St. Augustus!" Ethan said, disconnecting his phone from the music dock.

"Cole, do you think it would be all right if Ava and I put the map in our room?" Courtney asked, rushing back to the kitchen to retrieve it. "I hate leaving it here. Even if it doesn't work anymore, it would be safer with us."

"I think Ms. Krick would understand," he said. "I don't think the rest of campus is ready for anything we've seen."

Courtney put the rest of the papers into the cupboard and slipped the key into her pocket. She handed the map to me. "Here you are, roomie," she said.

"To the woods!" I declared, pointing my finger at the landing.

The others filed out, leaving me to close the door on the new space, where we would share many laughs in our final year at St. Augustus. I squinted back into the darkened room, as a flash of something at the window caught my eye.

"What is it, Ava?" Ethan asked, hanging back to wait for me on the top step.

"I thought I saw something at the window," I said.

"Izzy?" he asked. "I thought I saw him when my dad's car pulled up too but it was just a crow. I might never stop looking for him."

"Yeah," I said, confirming that there was nothing at the window with a quick glance. "I'm sure there are lots of owls in the woods."

"Being with you feels like home," he said, wrapping me into his embrace. "I missed you terribly this summer."

"I missed you, too." And I meant it. I could truly be myself when I was with him. He'd encouraged me to come clean with Dad about everything that had happened. My conscience was at peace and I had him to thank.

He kissed me deeply, sending a wave through me. I'd never lived in room sixty-five. Still, I was the luckiest girl on campus. Ethan's hand in mine tethered us to the moment as we followed our friends down the stairs and off to a new adventure. Together.

ACKNOWLEDGMENTS

When I sat down and wrote The Fountain on maternity leave with my third child, I never once thought that a few short years later I would be leaving my long-standing career as an executive in business to do all things writing, full time. Fans of The Fountain Series made that happen, and I've since become a book coach, a writing instructor, an editor and a public speaker in addition to writing.

I can't thank these fans enough for waiting so patiently (some not so patiently!) for this third and final installment in The Fountain Series. Wall of Wishes tries to answer all the questions I've ever been asked by readers about the world of St. Augustus and its quirky characters, and I hope it does justice to their imaginations!

I was overwhelmed by the amount of readers putting up their hands to help with the beta read. Thank you to Marj, Sandy, Brooke, Sophia, Abby, Mary, Angela, Marnie, Crystal, Nikki and Rob for taking the time to read this early draft and give feedback that helped give my characters stronger voices, and to all the others who offered their support. Truly, I feel very grateful to have so many who are invested in this series.

Thank you as well to Simon Rose, who has been involved at various stages of editing for all three books in The Fountain Series, Michell Plested, who has done the layout for all three books, Mark Leslie Lefebvre for his generosity with his amazing online skills, and Evil Alter Ego Press, who believed in this series and has been supportive throughout my journey.

My writing career wouldn't be possible without the support of my amazing family, and my writerly peeps – Avery Olive, Alisha Souillet, Danielle Jensen, all the writers who take the time to have coffee with me, the whole When Words Collide (WWC) crew, The gang at the Imaginative Fiction Writers Association (IFWA), my colleagues and students at Alexandra Writers' Association (AWCS), staff and fellow writers at the Young Alberta Book Society (YABS), my book coaching and editing clients, and my publicist, Mickey Mikkelson of Creative Edge. The support of this fabulous community makes my job the best.

Wall of Wishes may be the last installment of The Fountain Series, but for me, it's just the beginning. I am fortunate to have the amazing encouragement and support of my literary agent, Naomi Davis of Bookends Literary Agency. Thank you, Naomi, for believing in me and the stories I've written that have yet to see the light of day. Stay tuned everyone for more on what's yet to come…

ABOUT THE AUTHOR

Suzy Vadori

Young Adult Author

Suzy is a Book Coach, Editor, Public Speaker and the Calgary Bestselling Author of The Fountain Series (The Fountain, The West Woods, Wall of Wishes). This fantastical Young Adult Series has received two Aurora Nominations for Best Young Adult Novel, as well as Five Stars and a bronze medallion from Readers' Favorite Book Awards. She is represented by Naomi Davis of Bookends Literary Agency.

Suzy lives in Calgary, Canada with her husband and three children and is an involved member in the writing community. She is a Program Manager for Calgary's When Words Collide (WWC), teaches writing at Alexandra Writers' Centre Society (AWCS), and is a touring member of the Young Alberta Book Society (YABS). Suzy is also the founder of WriteIt! creative writing programs in schools.

Her book coaching business grew from the number of writers coming to her for writing tips, editing, marketing advice, project management and motivational support on their projects. She loves working with writers at all stages in many genres, including Non-Fiction, Memoir, Mystery, Thriller, Fantasy, Science Fiction, Women's Fiction, Romance, Middle Grade, Picture Books and of course, Young Adult. Suzy is pursuing her Advanced Book Coach Certification from Jennie Nash's Author Accelerator.

Suzy speaks to youth and adult audiences across Western Canada about how literacy can unlock doors and help you achieve your goals, whatever they may be. For more information on Suzy's books, book coaching, editing and event appearances, please visit suzyvadori.wordpress.com

Other Books in the Fountain Series

The Fountain

Careful what you wish for. It just might come true.

Ava Marshall, driven by a desire to learn more about her mother's past, moved across the country to attend St. Augustus. But her mom's secrets will have to wait, because she finds herself instantly hated for her family's connection to her new school and is forced to fight alone against a classmate who is setting Ava up to be expelled.

Fleeing campus, she takes a shortcut to her Gran's house through the forbidden West Woods and discovers a mysterious fountain that has the power to grant a wish and change it all. But can she live with the consequences? Or will she end up breaking every school rule and risking the love of her life to make it right...

The West Woods

Courtney Wallis wants nothing more than to escape St. Augustus boarding school. After uncovering a well-kept secret about the school's founder, Isaac Young, Courtney turns to the school's magic to convince her dad to let her leave. Things take a turn when she meets Cole, who lives in the nearby town of Evergreen. He gives her hope that things might not be so bad. However, the school's fountain has other ideas, and binds Courtney to her ambition, no matter the cost.

As Courtney struggles to keep the magic from taking over, she and her friends get drawn into the mystery woven into the school's fabric. Everything seems to lead back to the forbidden West Woods. Together, she and her friends seek out the spirits of the past to ask for help, and find themselves in much deeper than they'd bargained for. If they succeed, Courtney could be free of the magic. If they fail, she may never be the same.